She told herself that this massage was like any other…but it was a lie

Peggy's job required her to go closer to Troy, touch him, slide her fingers across his warm, damp skin and gently knead his flesh. But somehow she knew that if she did, there would be no turning back.

Peggy closed her eyes and tried to resist this particular impulse of hers…it was dangerous and it was a form of self-betrayal.

But Hot Sex Personified lay on her massage table in front of her—ready, willing and clearly able. And she hadn't had any in so long.

When she opened her eyes, Troy's gaze burned into hers, hot and amused and challenging on the most primal level. *Do me*, it said. *I'll make you scream.*

She grasped the sheet, the cool white cotton against her heated skin. Should she remove it, giving in to temptation? And could she live with herself if she didn't?

Dear Reader,

If you've ever visited Miami, Florida, you know it's a city that bares a lot of skin. In fact, it's safe to say that this city positively pulses with sex.

When I came up with the idea to set three books in a hip Miami salon and day spa, my editor suggested that we factor in the famous Miami nightlife, too. And so the idea for the AFTER HOURS miniseries was born: my salon and spa would stay open till midnight, serve wine and beer and function as a preparty hot spot for its clientele. What fun!

Doing the research for these three books was the best: I had to get a hot-stone massage, a great haircut and a pedicure—all in the name of business. Hard life, huh? I hope you enjoy reading Peggy and Troy's story as much as I enjoyed writing it.

All best,

Karen Kendall

P.S. I love hearing from readers! Write to me at www.KarenKendall.com or care of Harlequin Enterprises Ltd., 225 Duncan Mill Road, Don Mills, Ontario M3B 3K9, Canada.

Books by Karen Kendall

HARLEQUIN BLAZE
195—WHO'S ON TOP?*
201—UNZIPPED?*
207—OPEN INVITATION?*

*The Man-Handlers

KAREN KENDALL
Midnight Oil

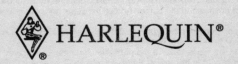

HARLEQUIN®

TORONTO • NEW YORK • LONDON
AMSTERDAM • PARIS • SYDNEY • HAMBURG
STOCKHOLM • ATHENS • TOKYO • MILAN • MADRID
PRAGUE • WARSAW • BUDAPEST • AUCKLAND

To my editor, Wanda Ottewell,
who is always a lot of fun to brainstorm with.

ISBN 0-373-79250-6

MIDNIGHT OIL

www.eHarlequin.com

Printed in U.S.A.

1

TROY BARRINGTON FELT like a pervert, sitting here in his car in a dark parking lot at 10:00 p.m. Either a pervert or a cop on a stakeout, except he didn't have any doughnuts or one of those cool police radios.

"What are you doing, Uncle Troy?" asked his eleven-year-old nephew, Derek, via cell phone.

He visualized the kid, tousled blond hair sticking out every which way and a chocolate stain on the Marlins T-shirt he liked to sleep in. His skateboard was probably at the end of his bed. "Just sitting out on the porch, smoking a cigar," Troy lied. He couldn't tell an eleven-year-old what he was really up to: spying on a bunch of people he didn't know but suspected were up to no good. He also couldn't tell Derek that one luscious redhead in particular made the stakeout a lot less boring than it could have been.

"Why are you still awake?" Troy asked, tearing his eyes away from her very interesting curves. "Huh? You should be in bed."

"Mom says cigars are bad for you," Derek told him, ignoring the question.

"They are. Terrible. But someone gave me this as a gift, and I didn't want to throw it away." It was true that he had a cigar in his glove box, from his friend Amos, whose wife had just had a baby girl. His old teammates were dropping like flies to wives and kids. He scrubbed a hand over his face. Hadn't it been just yesterday that they were all a bunch of rowdy, testosterone-crazed twentysomethings? He had no idea how he'd suddenly fallen into his midthirties, and still had no desire to settle down with a woman.

"Well," Derek said judiciously, "I guess that's okay, then. So did you fix the holes in your porch?"

"Nope. That's my weekend project, big guy. You wanna help?"

"Yeah! Can I really?"

"Uh-huh. If you promise to hang up the phone and go to bed now. I'll bet your mom doesn't know you're still up."

Guilty silence.

"Does she?"

"No. Are you gonna tell?"

"Not if you get to bed this minute. I'll talk to her tomorrow and see if I can pick you up Sunday morning, okay? After church."

"How 'bout before church?"

"*After* church. But good try."

His nephew sighed. "Can I use a power saw?"

"Absolutely not. But you can measure and mark for me, and help in other ways."

"Cool."

"Where are Danni and Laura?" Troy's twin nieces were twelve and played powder-puff football in his honor, which tugged at his heartstrings.

"They're spending the night with Lana Banana. That dumb girl."

"It's not nice to call her that."

"I know. Bye, Uncle Troy. Don't smoke any more cigars. Okay?"

"Yup." Troy hung up with a smile and refocused on the cute redhead.

His half sister's kids were one of the biggest reasons he'd moved to Miami—her creep husband had taken off and she was now a single mom. Frankly, Troy thought she was better off that way. Unfortunately, Derek and the girls weren't. They needed a decent male role model, and though Troy was certainly no angel, at least he could fake it for the kids.

From behind the windshield of his vintage Lotus, he squinted at Uncle Newt's strip mall. Correction: *his* strip mall. A month ago, at the reading of old Newt's will, Troy had suddenly become a slum lord.

Nine storefronts, most of them dark, stared back at him from his spot in a parking lot that had seen better days. The macadam was a faded gray and there were cracks everywhere. The lines demarking the car slots were barely visible during the day, and Troy wondered just how much money it cost to repave an entire lot. Damn. That would put another dent in his savings. And there'd been a few too many dents lately, one big one made by the kids' college funds. But Samantha would never be able to save enough, and the father was a deadbeat.

Troy tilted his head against the leather seat and leaned back to crack his neck, still training his gaze on the best storefront, the brightly lit one, dead center, with the largest expanse of plate glass. The one with all the laughing pretty girls inside, that redhead in particular, and a thousand bottles and jars of goop in the window. The one he wanted for his own business, a new sporting goods store—if he could break the tenants' lease.

After Hours, said the funky, squiggly script. A Salon and Day Spa. And in smaller letters, Open Till Midnight!

Inside, the place was self-consciously artsy, with an S-shaped reception desk, movable walls in pastel ice-cream colors and exotic glass lamps of different sizes and hues dangling over it all. There were filmy white curtains bracketing the windows, but the tenants never seemed to close them.

Yesterday, as he'd oh, so casually sauntered by, he'd spied a zebra floor cloth and a unicorn floor cloth, both of which appeared to be floating in an expanse of seawater from out here. When you got up close, you could see that the concrete floor had been textured and painted to resemble the ocean.

Fishy, thought Troy. *What kind of spa stays open until midnight? A spa that gives dirty massages to dateless, desperate men, that's what kind.* He smiled in the darkness. Because that sure violated the lease agreement.

His smile faded. At least, he'd been convinced of the spa's underhanded activities a couple of hours ago, when he first started watching the place. But to his disappointment, most of the clientele were women. And the two men who'd gone in had stayed up front, clearly visible in the well-lit windows while they got haircuts and laughed with the pretty girls over glasses of wine and beer.

Alcohol. What kind of spa serves drinks and blasts hip dance music? Troy could hear the music clearly from outside in his car, inspiring his unwilling fingers and toes to tap to it.

If he couldn't prove they were running a dirty massage parlor, then maybe he could get them on the liquor license. If they served alcohol, didn't they have to have one by law? Troy rubbed his jaw. Or was that only if they *sold* the drinks? No money was changing hands in there as far as he could see.

He continued to watch as the cute little redhead in the white lab coat bumped hips with a dark-haired girl in artsy clothes and rubber flip-flops. Red had serious curves, tempting and visible through the open coat. She also had sweet, kissable pale skin and a load of hair for a man to lose his hands in....

Okay, now he really *was* being a pervert. He was here on a business mission, not for a cheap thrill.

Red threw back her head and laughed, then spun 360 degrees on one foot. She wobbled as she stopped, though, and would have lost her balance if a tall, broad-shouldered Latino guy hadn't caught her by the elbow.

Aha! Where did *he* come from? Maybe, Troy thought hopefully, he'd been getting happy in the back. But no—he swung himself behind one of the manicure stations and…

Troy gaped. Surely that bruiser wasn't actually removing a woman's nail polish and then filing her nails? But he was. Where had the guy's balls gone hiding? Were they soaking in warm paraffin wax in the back?

He continued to feel like a Peeping Tom—and, oh, shit! The redhead squinted out the window again, looking directly at him. He ducked, sliding as low in the seat as he could go.

Troy stayed that way for two or three long minutes, barely breathing, his heart pumping fast. He was just about to ease upward again when a female voice spoke to him with deadly calm.

"There are laws against stalking in this state, you pathetic creep."

Troy looked up to find the redhead standing there, all five feet of her, aiming a container of Mace at his head.

"It's not what you think," he said, the words sounding lame to his own ears.

"Really. So what's up, then, big guy? You shopping for a dry cleaner at this hour of the night? Or did you figure you'd sleep in your car so you'd be first in line for hot doughnuts at 5:00 a.m.?"

"I'm *not* a stalker," he told her, straightening in his seat. "Or a rapist. But it's a really stupid move for you to come out here alone to confront one. What were you thinking?"

"Mace. It does a body good."

"Sweetheart, go back inside and don't ever try this

again. I could have that out of your hand and you pinned to the ground in about two seconds."

Her gaze drilled into his. In the dark he couldn't tell what color her eyes were, but he thought probably brown. Whatever color they were, they were gorgeous: almond-shaped, long-lashed and steely with determination.

"Yeah? I don't advise you to do that. Because I've called the cops, pervert, and they should be here within a minute or two. So if I were you I'd get the hell off of this property right now."

He really didn't need to be questioned by the police about his behavior. "Look, I'm telling you, this is not what you think. I'm not some kind of sicko." But Troy did as she suggested. He put the Lotus into gear and slowly drove away from her.

"And don't come back!" she shouted.

Great. Just great. Now is probably not the time to tell her she's hot—or ask her what she's doing next Saturday.

THE NEXT MORNING Troy awoke in his bed with a numb arm, a migraine and a persistent hard-on. Visions of the pissed-off redhead had flitted through his head all night, and in a lot of them she wore nothing but that lab coat, unbuttoned.

He'd been wasting his time the night before. He wished he'd gone to bed around the same time he'd forced Derek to do so. Besides the drinks and the weird late-night schedule, After Hours wasn't conducting any out-of-the-ordinary business, and he'd come close to being arrested for stalking. Damn it.

He focused on the extremely ugly brown-paneled wall of the furnished hovel he'd just purchased. The place dated from the early sixties and hadn't been remodeled since then. The scent of its elderly former resident, now dead, still hung in the air: a peculiar essence of Listerine, moth balls, old grease and musty carpet.

Troy swung his legs over the side of his bed and eyed the malfunctioning window-unit air conditioner sourly. Until he got this wreck of a place gutted and fixed up, he might be better off sleeping in his car.

The house had been the only halfway decent buy left in Miami's Coral Gables, and it was going to take a year of his time, a hundred contractors and a miracle of God to make it livable.

Troy shook his dead arm—it used to take a woman sleeping on it to make that happen—and made coffee one-handed as what felt like an army of ants ran from his wrist to his bicep. He yawned while something tickled at his barely functional brain.

Oh, right. Alcohol permit. He needed to check on that. If the tenants at the spa could be kicked out for something that simple, he'd be a happy guy.

He felt a little guilty as he drank coffee—black with one sugar—and did some research on the Internet to look into the laws. They'd all seemed so happy and energetic last night as he'd sat in the dark like a vulture, plotting to yank their storefront out from under them. A really nice guy, he was.

Hey, it's nothing personal. Just business.

Unfortunately, the Internet informed him that yes,

indeed, After Hours could legally serve beer and wine as long as they weren't selling it. Liquor required a license, but he'd seen no signs of them serving hard liquor.

Great. Since when had salons and spas turned into lightweight bars? He was obviously getting old.

Troy logged off gloomily and fried two eggs and three strips of bacon. He made toast. He regained use of his arm. And after a shower he drove back over to the strip mall to think about the problem in the light of day.

He parked the Lotus on the other side of the lot and walked by casually, peering in the door. Nobody was visible yet, but the salon would open in a few minutes. It looked spotless inside, and unfortunately there were no degenerates passed out on the floor after a night of partying. He frowned at the smaller gold letters on the door.

We're All About You!

Not, thought Troy. *If you were all about me, you and your male manicurist and your pampered princess clients would be outta here. My new sporting goods store would occupy that prime retail space. And you wouldn't be getting away with murder on the rent.*

What had Newt been thinking, when he'd signed all the tenants to bargain-basement rents and ten-year leases? Ten years! For chrissakes.

But Troy couldn't evict any of these people without cause, and he didn't particularly want to evict the ones in the smaller storefronts. Well, except maybe the nut bags in the Arrowroot Café, where they served chai or green tea instead of a decent cup of coffee and wouldn't make anything using dairy products, meat or wheat. Soy milk—ugh!

Wasn't it time to take back the planet from tree huggers and vegetarians? Was it too much to ask for a real cup of joe in the morning, a BLT for lunch and a steak after a long, hard day?

His gaze rested with more approval on the other restaurant in the strip mall. Benito's Bistro, an Italian place, seemed to be popular, judging by the constant stream of customers. So what if the owner shared his name with Mussolini—at least he wasn't a granola head.

Other businesses in the place included a mail and copy center, a dry cleaner, a gift shop and a small pharmacy. They were fine as far as Troy was concerned. He'd thought briefly about knocking out a wall between a couple of them and using the larger space for his new store, but he really wanted the large central one. And why lose two rents instead of one? Curiously, Newt hadn't charged After Hours higher rent, even though they had the biggest and best space. Why not?

His best guess was that Newt, a product of the Great Depression, had locked in the first paying customer to come along.

Troy had fond memories of fishing in the Everglades with Uncle Newt, but they had eaten everything they caught, and that meant *everything*. He'd almost gagged on the grilled salamander and he'd wondered if Newt ate the leftover bait when Troy went home to his parents....

His cell phone rang, interrupting his thoughts, and Troy flipped it open. "Hey, Jerry."

His attorney said, "Hey, yourself."

"Any luck finding a clause to break the lease?"

"I hate to disappoint you, but old Newt made sure the damn things were watertight. He didn't want anyone sliming out of their rent money."

Troy cursed.

"But if you can catch them on some violation, then you're good to proceed with eviction."

"What kind of violation?"

"Well, salons are notoriously regulated, and there are all kinds of little rules they might not be in compliance with. And remember, they have to have permits from the city for every single thing, from electrical outlets to drainage to cleanliness. See if you can get them on something. Maybe they snuck in an extra footbath somewhere, or a manicure table. Maybe they're not disinfecting the sink to standards. Or the pH in their shampoo ain't right. Hell, I don't know. You'll have to get in there and see."

"How am I supposed to recognize what's code and what's not? Can you fax me the regulations for Miami?"

"Fax them? The regs will be the size of the phone book. You asked me to keep your bill down."

Yes, Troy had. Jerry wasn't cheap. "Well, yeah, but I'm flying blind here! Can you overnight me a copy?"

"I'll get an intern on it. You'll have 'em by tomorrow morning."

"Thanks."

"How's the new house?"

"Peachy," Troy growled. Real estate had gone sky

high in South Florida, and Coral Gables was a primo location, so his three-bedroom shack was a great investment in spite of its appalling interior. Troy actually looked forward to the do-it-yourself challenge—it would distract him for the next year or so while he accustomed himself to not being part of a football organization. Until he got his sporting goods store going, he had way too much time on his hands.

Troy was also going to have to accustom himself to being on a budget. As a former strong safety for the Jacksonville Jaguars, he wasn't used to that. But the stock market had been performing poorly, he had his nieces and nephew to think about and he'd lost his coaching job in Gainesville after the team went on a losing streak. *Just business, nothing personal.*

In a heartbeat he'd gone from being a big cheese in Jacksonville to a…cheese doodle. He was unaccustomed to being a nobody and, frankly, it abraded his ego. Hell, nobody in South Florida even recognized him, much less asked for an autograph.

But beyond that, Troy wanted to control his own financial future: he was sick of being jerked around like a puppet by various football organizations, just as he was sick of women who used him for his connection to them. It was time to change all of that.

He considered hiring Jerry's intern to snoop around After Hours, but decided to suck it up and do it himself. He'd park in the back, and hopefully the curvy redhead wouldn't recognize him in daylight. All she'd really seen was a head in a car.

He ended the call with Jerry, cutting off his banter about the Miami Heat and the unbearable mosquitoes this time of year. At a cool three hundred an hour, Jerry loved to have long conversations with his clients and then bill them for the pleasure. Once, Troy would have played along, but not now. Jerry could discuss free throws and insect larvae at somebody else's expense.

Troy glared again at After Hours and the hundreds of foo-foo bottles and jars in the window. Snooty, tooty-fruity place.

He pictured canoes, camping equipment, mountain bikes in that window. Hiking boots and parkas, wet suits and surfboards. Rugged, outdoorsy stuff.

He pictured a gathering place for sports-minded, manly men. Hell, maybe he'd install a wide-screen TV and some seating and serve beer himself! If the Pretty Palace could, then he sure as hell could. The vision grew in his head until he saw himself presiding over a retail version of *Cheers*. He'd have company all day and everyone would know his name…he'd be, if not a big cheese, a medium one.

Troy gave a mighty yawn and thanked the Guy Upstairs that he didn't have to play Peeping Tom again tonight. Being sleep deprived made him cranky.

But no matter what it took, he'd get this silly salon and spa off his property. He just had to get inside the damn place and figure out how.

2

"PEG," THE RECEPTIONIST reasoned at After Hours Salon and Spa, "how are you going to meet Mr. Right when you won't go out?"

Peggy Underwood, the spa's manager and massage therapist, rolled her eyes. "I'm going to buy him from a pet store, already housebroken." She no longer believed in Mr. Right. She was pretty sure that he'd been dreamed up by Disney, like Donald and Goofy and Mickey.

"Peggy! You're so cynical."

"Yeah. And I refuse to apologize for it. I told you about the weirdo staring at us from the parking lot last night."

Shirlie looked uncomfortable. "He was probably harmless, but I'm glad you got rid of him."

Peg twisted off the cap of a body mist and sprayed some into the air. She sniffed. "Nice. Breezy. Gardenias." She squirted some under each arm of her white lab coat, recapped the bottle and stuck it onto one of the spa's shelves.

Shirlie laughed and tossed her short blond curls. Peg looked at them with envy. Why hadn't she been born tall, thin and blond, instead of short, curvy and carrottopped?

"Come on," Shirlie urged. "This new club is fab. Hot men, cold drinks, great music!" She kept on blandishing. Shirlie was twenty-two, fresh-faced and eternally optimistic.

Peggy herself was twenty-nine, cynical and currently cranky, even though she kept reminding herself that she didn't like cranky people. "I think what you mean, Shirl, is gay or gruesome men, cheap, watered-down vodka and lip-synching to the latest prepackaged boy band. I love you, hon, but I think I'll pass."

Men were of no interest to Peggy for the next fifty-two weeks; she was committed to finding her center. Before the year was out, she'd be floating in a state of total balance between mind, body and spirit. She'd taken up meditation, she was reading about Buddhism and she not only gave massages and treatments but underwent them regularly herself.

Peg popped the lids off some new erotic lipsticks from Sugar Lips and inspected them. Nice. High quality. Very kissable. The company was new, and she'd only recently discovered it.

Since the image for After Hours was oriented to sexy, evening fun she'd tested one and ordered some immediately. They glided on beautifully and tasted delicious.

She chose three different flavors and drew stripes of them on the inside of her wrist: one cinnamon raspberry, one pink and one deep slut red. "Hmm. Try this on, okay?" She tossed the red one to Shirlie.

She tested the pinky cinnamon one on herself, applying the Ride Him Raspberry generously.

Then she lip-synched—puckered up against an invisible microphone—to the Brazilian pop song on the sound system. She moonwalked to the reception desk while Shirlie laughed again. Peg scooped up a box behind the desk and cushioned it against her stomach as she gyrated back to the shelves.

Producing a utility knife from her pocket, she slit open the box with a dramatic, pseudosexual gesture and tore it open as if it were a man's shirt.

Shirlie shook her head at her and tossed the lipstick back, her mouth now fire-engine red. Peg evaluated the color, nodded and then continued to stock new products on the spa's curvy modern shelves, blinking under the bright halogen lighting.

Her heart-shaped, freckled face and red hair competed with bottles, jars and tubes for reflection space in the mirrors behind the shelves. Her skin was almost as pale as the white tips of her chipped French manicure. What had possessed her to move to sunny Miami?

Oh, right: the ability to spend more time outdoors, under an inch of SPF 30 sunscreen instead of two inches of wool.

"You have to get back into the swing of things sometime," Shirlie urged. "Not all men are like Eddie."

Ugh. Her ex-fiancé. Steroid-popping jock. Compulsive gambler. Borderline alcoholic. Cheap, lying bastard! She'd moved down here from Connecticut to make a new start.

Peg's hand tightened around a tube of hair gel so hard that it spit off the loose top and plopped some product onto the floor. She looked down at the mess, reached for a tissue and mopped it up.

"You deserve so much better than that," Shirlie said. "And trust me, you have a better chance of finding it— him—while wearing a cute little miniskirt on a dance floor than wearing your baggy, ice-cream-stained pajamas on your couch."

"Hey!" Peggy said. "There are no ice-cream stains on my pj's. I wash them regularly. And besides," she added, "since they can now clone sheep, it's got to be a snap to clone a single-cell organism like a man. I'm thinking we'll be able to order men from a catalogue within about five years. I could be really into that."

Shirlie wrinkled her nose. "That would take all the fun out of life. What about the thrill of the chase?"

Poor thing. She was still young enough that she got excited about the whole silly mating dance. "What thrill? Shirlie, I'd get a huge charge out of just ordering up a man without the burping or farting gene. Or the beer-gut gene! Can you imagine the possibilities? You might even be able to special-order one with an on-off switch. Or even better, an erect-limp switch!"

"Eeuuwww." Shirlie's expression was priceless.

Peg stuffed an unruly curl behind her ear and said, "Oh, right. You're still too young to have had more than a five-minute-long relationship, so maybe none of these issues has come up. Or, uh, refused to come up, as the case may be." She produced some fiendish laughter. "Mwah-ha-ha-ha, my pretty! Nothin' but good times ahead." She winked.

"Peggy, I wouldn't date a...nonstarter."

Peg scooped more bottles and tubes out of a box, her tongue in her cheek. "Well, here's the thing, honey. You don't always *know* at first. For example, take my advice and stay far, far away from any guy who's on steroids."

"Oh, my God! You don't mean that Eddie..."

Peg nodded. "I could write a book called *Limp Lovin'*. The man popped so many pills that his dong had turned to linguine."

Shirlie's expression was priceless. "Hey, at least you know he wasn't cheating on you, right?"

Peg choked. "True. Not without a Popsicle stick and some electrical tape, anyway." She didn't feel in the least bad about revealing her ex's dark secret, since the creep had actually swapped the stone in her engagement ring for a cubic zirconia. Which brought her to another piece of advice for Shirlie. "And, hon, take it from me—don't date any guy who shows an affinity for gambling."

"O-kaaaay."

"Then there are the ones who hate women, even though they like to have sex. And the ones who have inferiority complexes and have to bring you down so they can feel superior. And worse, there are—"

Shirlie clapped her hands over her ears and moaned. "Stop! Look, maybe it *is* a good idea for you to stay home tonight. I just want to go dancing and have a good time, Miss Wet Blanket."

Peg grinned at her. "Yeah, well, it's better than being Mrs. Wet Blanket, married to a guy who's so cheap that his wallet creaks when he has to open it. Or—"

Shirlie was beginning to look a little wild-eyed when the door to After Hours opened and in walked The Man. Her eyes went from wild to glazed over within a nano-second.

Peg observed this while running her own eyes over The Man. He was six feet, two inches of gym-terrorized perfection, she had to give him that. His wide, solid torso formed a perfect V as it tapered into his slim waist, which was the only thing slim about him. He had the biceps of a young Arnold Schwartzenegger, shoulders that made even Peg want to cram a fist into her mouth and long, lean-looking legs. She couldn't see his backside, but she'd be willing to bet that it was Grade A prime beef.

The Man smiled at her, displaying even white teeth.

Just as a spark of sexual awareness shot through her belly and zoomed lower, she recovered her mental capacity. *Steroids,* she sang to herself. *The guy is so bulked up he looks like he's made of rubber. He'd bounce if you threw him on the pavement. And he's probably a knucklehead, to boot.*

Peg pulled her white lab coat closed against his gaze. There was something vaguely familiar about him, which disconcerted her. She didn't like his air of cool appraisal either—he stepped in as if he owned the place.

Shirlie beamed at The Man and got an instant case of the nervous babbles. "Hi, welcome to After Hours! I mean, I know it's not after hours right now, it's regular daytime business hours, but After Hours is the name of the salon and spa since we're open 9:00 a.m. to midnight. Isn't that fabulous? New marketing concept. Most people don't have time to leave work and come during the day, so we get them to come at night."

"Oh," said The Man, "I'm not particular about when I come." He grinned at Peg.

She narrowed her eyes, but she couldn't find a trace of innuendo or sarcasm in his voice.

Shirlie's blue eyes widened and she squirmed. "Uh, *arrive* at night. Make evening appointments. I didn't mean, well, you know…" Shirlie blushed fire. "I didn't mean anything by—I just meant— Oh, God, just shoot me. But by the way, I'm Shirlie!"

Peg cringed for her.

The Man blinked, bit back laughter and finally said politely, "Nice to meet you, Shirlie."

"You have an appointment for a massage?" She scanned the book, looking very much as if she'd like to close her face in it and die.

He shook his head and opened his mouth to speak, but the babbles took hold of her again. "You're here to have your back waxed, then! Of course. Don't be embarrassed—lots of men have your problem. We wax backs all the time. My brother has come here for that. No shame in it at all—"

"Actually," The Man said, "I'm here to—"

"Your bikini area, then?" Shirlie blurted.

"God, no!" He looked alarmed.

Peggy decided that it was time she stepped in, to rescue both Shirlie and The Man from any more awkwardness. "What can we help you with?" she asked.

"I was, uh…" He looked up at the ceiling tiles, of all places. And along the baseboards. He squinted into the back of the salon, gazing…under the sinks?

Peggy didn't know what to make of him. Then he stuck his foot in his mouth.

"Listen," he said. "Do any straight guys come here?"

Unbelievable. Peg couldn't help it. She snorted.

He looked at her sharply.

She cleared her throat. "Sorry. Just getting over a cold. Yes, plenty of straight guys come here. Your masculinity is safe on our premises."

"Are you making fun of me?" he asked.

Oh, hell. Yes, I was, and it was wrong, and it's certainly not good business to do that. "No, no. Not at all." She gave him her best smile. "We're running a special right now on spa packages, and as the manager, I can offer you twenty-five percent off. Would you be interested in booking our Qu—uh, *King* package? It's a combination of a sea salt body scrub and wrap, a hot stone massage and a warm mud bath. Very relaxing and rejuvenating—and men, straight men, get this package all the time."

"Sounds great," The Man said, looking uninterested and still inspecting everything but the decor, which usually riveted first-time visitors since it was so splashy and contemporary. Orchid, sea-foam green, yellow and pink walls surrounded übermod furniture and funky floor cloths.

After dark, the spa's lighting, music and atmosphere created almost a nightclub feel, where clients could have a cocktail or two while getting their nails or hair done. Part of Shirlie's job was to mix drinks after 5:00 p.m.

The idea was that the spa functioned as a relaxing, fun preparty spot where clients could start their evenings while being pampered and polished.

"Would you like to book your package all at once," Peg asked, "or in three separate treatments?"

The Man hesitated for a moment. "Three separate treatments, please," he said.

"All right." Since Shirlie wasn't responding to the verbal cues, Peg took the appointment book from her apparently nerveless hands and flipped through the pages. "When would you like to come in?"

"Uh, tomorrow? Say, around six or seven?"

She scanned the book. Their part-time massage therapist was off tomorrow. She'd have to take the appointment herself. "Seven o'clock all right?"

"That'll be fine, thanks." He continued to scan the premises. What was he, an engineer? Again, he didn't seem interested in the design, the multicolored walls or the distressed, hand-painted cement floor.

He did seem interested in *her*—she could feel it in his gaze—but it was as if he didn't want to be.

There was something about him that she didn't trust, though she couldn't put her finger on why. And why did he seem familiar? It wasn't just that his casual, cocky, muscular stance reminded her of Eddie.

Don't be ridiculous, she told herself. *There's nothing sinister in a guy signing up for a sea salt scrub.*

She tried not to think about the fact that tomorrow

she'd be running her bare hands all over those broad shoulders of his, that smooth, tanned muscle. Her body went on full, red-hot alert, which wasn't in the least professional.

Shirlie was still pinned in the receptionist's chair by the visual force of the man, riveted by that butt of his as he strode to the door. Was that a trickle of drool at the corner of her mouth?

The butt was indeed Grade A prime. And his chinos fit him just right. The Man's back muscles rippled as he opened the door, and both Peg and Shirlie sighed as he walked through it and let it close behind him. God, what was wrong with the pair of them? This was Miami—they saw male models all the time.

It wasn't until he'd disappeared from sight that Peg realized she'd forgotten to get his name and phone number. Had she really been lecturing Shirlie in that smug, worldly way just a few minutes ago? She herself was just as bad!

"What do you think he looks like with his clothes off?" Shirlie asked reverently. "Did you catch his name?"

Peg shook her head sheepishly. "No, but I'll be the one doing his sea salt scrub tomorrow, so—"

"Shut-*up*-no-you-are-not!"

"Yep."

"Some people have all the luck. I'm going to get my license, I swear."

"Believe me, not all your customers will look like that. There are some people you do not want to see naked. Case in point, Pugsy Malloy. I close my eyes when I have to do Pugsy."

Shirlie sighed. "Yeah, but I think I'd sign up for five Pugsys if I could have just one what's-his-name."

Peggy laughed. "Okay, Miss Babble. Wipe the slobber off the reception desk."

Shirlie wrinkled her nose. "I did babble, didn't I? I'm so embarrassed. But you were drooling, too! Don't deny it."

"I did not drool," said Peg with dignity. "I just salivated a little."

Judging from her face, a horrifying possibility had just occurred to Shirlie. "You don't think...you don't think that guy does steroids, do you? I mean, it would be a crying shame if—"

Peggy pursed her lips. "Judging by his body, I can't say I'd be surprised." She began to flatten the cardboard box that had held the new products.

"Tomorrow at eight, you have to give me a full report! Plus his name and number."

"Shirlie, I'm not likely to see that part of him. I do work with a sheet, hon."

"Oh, c'mon! Can't you take a little sneak peek? Just for me?"

"No," said Peg, laughing. "That's not ethical and you know it." She tossed the flattened box into the trash.

"Who said anything about ethics? I just don't want to waste my time if he's hung like a garden slug."

Peg shook her head. "Shirl, you're impossible. Go dancing tonight. Get it out of your system. Do everything I wouldn't do, and have fun. You know I adore you, but I cannot check out a customer's equipment on the sly."

"Can you step on the sheet *accidentally?* And, hey, do you have a camera phone? Or you could text message me from the back room—"

"*No.* I'm going to lunch now. Can I get you anything while I'm out? A foot-long hot dog, perhaps?" She laughed as Shirlie threw a wad of paper at her, and ducked out the door.

Peggy walked down the block to a local sandwich shop, grimacing at the heat and humidity of Miami in May. Unfortunately, her seven-o'clock appointment the next day had now started to assume a significance of epic proportions. The question was, would her client's significant proportions also be epic?

3

AT FIVE MINUTES TO SEVEN, Peggy put a William Ackerman new age CD into the treatment room's stereo system and hit the play button. She lit an imported French candle—Japanese-quince scented—and spread plastic, clean white towels and a fresh sheet on her massage table.

She looked around the room, satisfied that it was soothing and calming. The walls were a delicate pale blue, with a mural of trees, grass and rolling hills on one side and a beach on the other. Marly, the salon's hair-stylist, had painted them, plus a mural of an open window on one end, since the real thing was absent. The window "looked into" a cozy living room, so that the client felt as if he or she was being treated in an outside garden bower. They'd added a real window box at the painted sill and planted silk flowers in it. The effect was charming and magical—as well as soothing.

For some odd reason, butterflies had invaded Peggy's stomach. She emerged from the treatment room and rounded the corner, walking down the apple-green hallway and then into the hall near the front of the spa, wiping her palms quickly on her lab coat as she heard the door of After Hours open and close. A deep voice announced that Troy Barrington was here for his seven o'clock appointment.

Troy. The Man's name, at last. It fit him: one no-nonsense syllable, and masculine in the extreme. Peg still couldn't believe she'd forgotten to ask it yesterday.

She braced herself to go out and get him, tying her hair back into a ponytail since it was best not to shed on the clientele. She buttoned her lab coat and then pulled a tube of Sugar Lips Ride Him Raspberry from her pocket. She dabbed some on her lips while simultaneously scolding herself for primping. She'd sworn off men for a year, remember? Plus, the guy was an über-jock, for God's sake, and she'd sworn off *jocks* for life.

Peg walked into the reception area. She should have brought a tissue to wipe the drool from Shirlie's chin. The girl's cheeks were flushed, and she kept rearranging a vase of flowers, managing to snap half the blooms and leaves off them.

Peggy remembered a time when hot men had made her nervous. But that was *so* long ago, before she'd learned that they were all schmucks. The butterflies she'd felt in her stomach? *Puh-lease.* It was just hunger: she wanted her dinner.

"Nice to see you again, Troy." Peg held out her hand to him. See? It wasn't shaking the tiniest bit.

Troy had been inspecting the display of erotic lipsticks with a raised brow, paying special attention to Whip Me Cream.

He turned to greet her and she felt dwarfed by his sheer size: not all height, but breadth, too. Somehow, with the reception counter between them, he hadn't seemed quite this big yesterday.

He wrapped huge, warm fingers around hers and clasped gently. "Hi." He gestured with his head toward the lipsticks. "Interesting products you got there." He wore a knowing grin.

She felt a jolt at the contact, and a flush started at her neck, as if she were a teenager. "They're great. The next Smashbox or Hard Candy, but more fun."

His amusement faded to puzzlement.

"Never mind. Girl stuff." She smiled. "My name is Peggy, and I'll be doing your sea salt scrub this evening. Can I get you something to drink? Wine? Beer? Sparkling water?"

"Bottled water would be great," he said, releasing her hand.

She nodded in approval. He cared about his body. Peg was torn about the alcohol policy in the spa. On the one hand, it brought them clients and helped them keep the fun, partylike atmosphere at night. On the other, alcohol didn't really have much to do with total mind-body-spirit fitness. It muddled the mind, slowed the body and wasn't great for the spirit, either, after the initial high.

However, alcohol had been great for business. Simply amazing how a drink or two loosened up wallets and led to further treatments. A regular pedicure became a spa pedicure; a simple facial led to the purchase of two hundred dollars' worth of products, and so on.

"Just follow me." She led Troy to the treatment room and showed him the table, though he seemed to be looking at everything in the room but that. He was intense about it, too.

It was almost as if he were some kind of corporate spy, checking out their premises so that he could set up a competing business. She didn't know what to think.

"Have you ever had a sea salt scrub before?" she asked him.

He shook his head. "No, can't say as I have. Why is there a drain in the floor here?"

"This used to be the only wet room we had," Peggy explained. "So we had what's called a Vichy shower mounted over the treatment table. But now we have four wet rooms surrounding central locker rooms over there—" she pointed to a set of double doors "—so the showers are centralized. When we're done here, you'll just walk into the men's area, find an unoccupied shower and rinse off."

He nodded.

"Through the doors and to the right, there's a set of teak shelves where you'll find folded spa robes and clean towels. Here's a locker key—" Peggy handed it to him "—so you can store your things securely.

"Go ahead and take a quick shower just to get your skin moist, and then come on back in here. You can hang your robe on the back of the door. Then just lie down on your stomach and cover yourself with the folded sheet at the foot of the table. Do you have any questions?"

"So when did you make all these improvements to the place?" Troy asked casually.

"Recently. Just last year, when Alejandro relocated what was his mother's salon and expanded into a day spa, too. I came onboard as the manager and massage therapist only about three months ago."

"Alejandro is your…?"

"Business partner and a childhood friend."

"Oh, so you grew up in Miami?"

"No, I grew up mostly back East. But we lived here for a few years. Alejandro's been here all his life, though, and we've always kept in touch." Peg moved toward the door. "I'm going to get your water now, okay? Go ahead and make yourself comfortable and I'll be back in a couple of minutes."

She exited and tried not to think about Troy Barrington unbuttoning his shirt, unbuckling his belt, stepping out of his jeans. Tried not to think about the expanse of muscle that would greet her when she walked back through the door. She was a professional, after all.

Peggy walked to the kitchenette and got one of the spa's tall, apple-green plastic cups from a cabinet, added a few ice cubes to it and began to fill it with bottled water from the fridge. She caught sight of herself in the steel microwave door and as usual hated her freckled, pug nose. Not the kind of schnoz that got a man fantasizing.

"Hey!" she said aloud. "I don't *want* men fantasizing. Mind, body, spirit. No guys."

"What's that, hon?" Marly Fine, the spa's hairstylist and muralist, walked up behind her and dumped out the remnants of her green tea. Her glossy black hair hung in a loose French braid down her back and she'd eaten off all her lip gloss, along with part of her lip liner, too. Despite this, Marly was true to her last name: fine. Tall and willowy and ethereal, with deep blue-green eyes and unfairly olive skin.

"Mind, body, spirit. Impulse control. Balance in all things," said Peggy, feeling like the Pillsbury Doughboy in a red wig beside her. She needed to get her butt running again, instead of just coaching kids to do it from the sidelines. But no matter how much she ran or starved, her legs would always be short and thick compared to Marly's.

"Right, mind, body, spirit." The hairstylist batted Peg's ponytail playfully. "I hear you have a hottie under your sheet right now."

"Is Shirlie still panting out there?"

"Yes." Marly's expression was amused. "And she swears she's seen the guy before, in the news or on TV or something. What does he do?"

Peg shrugged. "Beats me. All I've done is ask him what he wants to drink and point him toward the men's locker room."

"Well, once you've got him kneaded to jelly under your magic hands, try to figure out the mystery. She's going to drive me crazy." Marly got another tea bag out of a canister and stuck her mug, full of water, into the microwave.

Peggy liked green tea, too, but preferred it cold, straight from the refrigerator. "Okay. So what's your evening look like?"

"I'm doing highlights on Candy Moss right now. She's had two glasses of wine and is giggling for no apparent reason under the dryer. Then a couple of updos for some gala in Coconut Grove. And last a simple cut and blow-dry. I should be able to leave early tonight."

"Lucky you."

"That reminds me, though—would you be able to wax a client's eyebrows after you're done with the hottie?"

"Sylvia can't do it?" Sylvia was their aesthetician.

"She can, but this woman doesn't like her—she over-plucked her last time."

"Oh, okay. Sure." Peg headed for the exit. "Good luck with Candy after glass of wine number three, okay?" They really weren't supposed to give the customers more than two drinks, but sometimes it was hard to cut them off.

Marly laughed. "Thanks."

Peggy headed down the hallway and knocked on the treatment room door.

"Come in," Troy said. He was lying facedown on the table, with the sheet draped over his lower half.

Peggy swallowed hard at the sight of his broad, smooth, tanned back and powerful biceps and triceps. She'd had a feeling his body was gorgeous underneath the simple cotton knit shirt.

"Here's your water," she said.

Troy propped himself up on his elbows and accepted it with thanks, flashing a chest that reminded her of Brad Pitt's in, appropriately enough, *Troy*. It segued into a perfectly flat abdomen sporting a six-pack of trained, hard muscle, and her knees went disgustingly weak at the sight.

Jock. Eddie. Jocks suck. Be true to own mind, body, spirit. Impulse control.

Still she stared at Troy's chest while he drank his water, until he quirked an eyebrow. "Have you spotted something important to science?"

"What?" She flushed. "Uh, no. Let's get started, okay?"

He flashed her a quizzical grin and she realized, mortified, that she'd sounded as if she was in a hurry to touch him. Worse, he didn't seem surprised. Egotistical jerk.

He set his cup down on a side table within reach and relaxed again on the table.

"Music okay?" she asked in crisp tones as she prepared the salt scrub. She added just a touch more shower gel to it so it would glide onto his skin smoothly. She mixed it with a wooden tongue depressor, the same thing a doctor would use with patients.

"It's very…uh, peaceful," he said. "So how long have you been doing this, Peggy?"

Let the small talk begin. "For about five years."

"What did you do before?"

"I got out of college, waitressed and bartended for a couple of years, then tried to work for my brother, Hal, as an account manager—which was boring beyond belief."

"You don't like a nine-to-five office environment?"

"God, no."

Peggy filled her hands with the salt scrub and warmed it a bit before spreading it over Troy's shoulders and upper back. "I'm more of an outdoors person, believe it or not." She laughed a little self-consciously, smoothing her hands in circles over his skin.

He groaned softly, and she was pleased that it felt good to him.

"But I'm not really artistic enough to become a landscape architect," she continued, "and I don't have any desire to dig ditches…so here I am. I do this and also coach a powder-puff football team on the side."

Troy lifted his head. "You're kidding—my twelve-year-old twin nieces are on a powder-puff team."

Her hands stopped. "Twins? Their names aren't Danni and Laura, are they?"

"Yes! Blond? Smart mouths?"

"That's them! I coach them Tuesday, Thursday, Saturday at the Woodward School. They're really good, too."

"Yeah, don't I know it. I'm the one who taught them to throw a ball. I used to play strong safety for the Jacksonville Jaguars."

Ugh. Football player, worst species of the genus Jock. She should have known. "Of course—that's where I've heard your name," Peg said politely. "Shirlie, our receptionist, was convinced that you were some celebrity…she'll be so psyched that she was right."

"Celebrity? Nah." But he looked pleased. "You tell her I'm just a broken-down old ball player."

He certainly didn't look broken-down to Peggy. He didn't feel broken-down, either, as she polished his body with the salt scrub and a loofah mitt. She was so close to him as she worked that she could smell the faint after-shave on his jaw and the essence of Dial soap on his skin.

The gel she'd mixed with the salt had a sweet grape-fruit scent. Imported from France, they'd just gotten it in last month and it was very popular. She smoothed it into his skin, exfoliating and massaging, and thought about the odd intimacy of her job. Most of the time, if anyone was uncomfortable, it was the client, unused to the touch of a stranger.

But right now she herself was discomfited, and fighting the urge to…she didn't know exactly. Rub her face against the smooth skin of his back, or even hike up her lab coat and skirt and sit astride him, feel him between her thighs.

To distract herself from the renegade thoughts, she forced herself to focus on his nieces, white-blond Danni and dishwater-blond Laura.

"Laura's an amazing place kicker and Danni throws one of the tightest spirals I've ever seen," she said, trying not to be fascinated with the corded muscle in Troy's forearms. The man might have retired from the playing field, but he still worked out.

"Yeah." He chuckled. "Danni's got quite an arm. And she's fierce, too! Laura's not as aggressive, but she's all about precision. I started working with them on my visits when they were about six, I think. So how did you get into football? I know a lot of women who watch it, but not many who play it or coach it."

Peggy didn't know exactly what to say. She had a love-hate relationship with football. How did she explain, without sounding pathetic, that she'd started learning it to get her father's attention after he left? That she was so good that all the Little League teams had been thrilled to have her—until high school, when suddenly she was suspect.

"Oh, I don't know," she said, working her way down to his lower back muscles and getting perilously close to the sheet covering his glutes. "I was a real tomboy, I guess, and used to play with the neighborhood kids. I worked at it. I was good. I watched it all the time on TV—thought it was a lot more interesting than making Barbie kiss Ken. And my dad was really into football."

She didn't mention that she'd loved to tackle people, that it had helped with all the pent-up anger and frustration she'd felt over her parents' divorce. At first she'd blamed her mom for not being nice to Dad, for making him want to leave. Then she'd found out why Mom wasn't nice: Dad had a girlfriend on the side.

"Yeah? So what's your favorite team?" Troy asked, his voice trailing into something like a deep purr as she firmly massaged the muscles on either side of his spine.

"Dolphins. Dan Marino was my hero."

"Yeah? Mine, too." Troy turned his head toward her and smiled. "Watching the guy run with those bad knees was like seeing paint dry, but man, his passing game was incredible."

Peggy nodded. "Quick release, amazing accuracy, tight spirals. Good thing he had Mark Clayton and Mark Duper to pass to."

"I can see my nieces are in good hands. Speaking of

which—" Peggy moved from his back to his thighs, and he edged them apart a bit "—so am I. They teach you how to do this in some special school?"

"Yes."

"Well, I'll bet you got all As."

"Let's just say I did better at this than at trig and calculus."

His legs were covered in a light sprinkling of coarse hair, and his thighs were packed with muscle, as were the calves. She applied more scrub and worked it in over every inch that wasn't private, right down to his feet and each toe.

"Okay," she said finally. "You can turn over now."

He rolled onto his back, holding the sheet in place over him.

She did her very best not to look at that area, even though Shirlie's questions came tumbling back into her mind. *Do you have a camera phone? Can't you just accidentally step on the sheet? You can text message me from the back....*

Peggy bit her lip to keep from laughing.

"What's the dimple for?" Troy asked, just as her humor vanished on seeing his chest and shoulders again.

She turned away for another handful of the salt scrub. God, the man was gorgeous. And this—she applied the scrub to his skin, trying not to meet his eyes—this was even more intimate.

"Dimple?" He had flat, coppery nipples, and she avoided them, not wanting the salt to irritate the more sensitive areas of his skin.

"You get a dimple, only on the left, when you're trying not to smile. It's cute."

"Um, thanks." She worked salt scrub into his left bicep and tricep groups, using both hands to span the muscles. She swallowed as she met his eyes, which were gray green like stormy seawater and set off by his tanned skin.

His lips held a devilish curve as she bent over him and worked her way over his chest, across his rib cage, down his abdomen. He had an old scar there, she noticed, and as her fingers drew near it he murmured, "Appendicitis at fifteen."

"Painful," she said.

"Mmm."

She'd reached the limits of the sheet and couldn't help looking right smack into the center of it. Not that she was sharing with Shirlie, but she didn't need to accidentally step on the sheet to tell that there was nothing wrong with his personal equipment. Troy Barrington, she decided, had never been on steroids.

4

TROY RELAXED on the massage table, relieved that Peggy hadn't connected him with the "stalker" in the parking lot.

She'd been quite the little scrapper then, and he loved her hands on him now. They were small, white and soft, just like her, but they possessed an unexpected strength—and she radiated competence from every pore.

Competent, confident women turned him on like nothing else. Women who didn't need him and didn't look up to him; women who weren't groupies or sluts. Cool women who were a challenge without being bitchy—those were the ones Troy found irresistible.

Troy had seen all types, having been a professional ball player. He'd been chased by hundreds of beautiful women, very few of them interested in who he was as a person. They just flocked to the outer package: the muscular guy with the glamorous, well-paying job and the great car—not that most of them even recognized what the Lotus was. "Why don't you drive a nice car, like a Porsche, instead of that old thing?" one girl had asked him. That had been their first and last date.

Troy had no regrets about leaving Jacksonville or

Gainesville—well, besides his new, lowly status of Head Cheese Doodle and Nobody. It was a little lonely starting over, but it felt good. He had no baggage in Miami. No big reminders of the selfish, hedonistic guy he'd been for years. He was a new man, shouldering new responsibilities, and he was strangely enthusiastic about them. For the first time his life would have meaning to someone other than himself.

As Peggy's hands slid over his skin, buffing him with the coarse salt stuff, he felt half relaxed and half energized. The cute redhead with the dimple was genuinely into football. The girl knew her stuff. Even coached his nieces…. It was a small world.

He felt her hands stop at the sheet covering his privates and wished he could throw it off. Though come to think of it, he really didn't want his knob polished with sea salt—it might be a tad painful. He wouldn't mind rinsing off the stuff and then pulling her on top of him, though.

Troy entertained himself by imagining once again that she was naked under that spiffy little white lab coat. That her full breasts were straining against the buttons and that maybe she had a Brazilian wax job with just the skinniest strip of red hair covering her down there.

He groaned as Peggy went to work on the tops of his thighs, and was forced to push his fantasies away before things got embarrassing. A folded sheet couldn't hide a determined arousal, and he shouldn't be thinking this way about his nieces' coach, for chrissakes.

To relieve himself, he pictured her instead in a hairnet, à la cafeteria lady. Then he added a flannel night-gown and matching robe with giant blue cabbage roses all over them. He smeared her face with cold cream for good measure.

Ah, that was better: the pressure in his groin subsided.

Peggy, oblivious to these changes in her appearance, simply did her job. And with her hands all over his body this way, Troy found it hard to remember why he was here in the first place: to scope out the spa for code violations.

Okay, she'd mentioned that the showers were new and they'd undergone extensive renovations. There should be city permits for all of that on file.

Oh, damn, that feels good! He almost drooled with gratitude. No, no, where was he?

Oh, yeah. There should also be inspection reports by officials to determine that everything was built to code. What he needed to do was somehow research each and every change to the building in the last two years....

Peggy's wonderful hands stopped—

No, no! Don't stop, please don't stop. Touch me just a little farther south. There's a toy surprise there, honey.

—and she announced that he should go and shower now. He thanked her and regretfully got up after she'd exited. Troy pulled on the cotton waffle-weave robe again and headed for the state-of-the-art showers to rinse off.

He stood under the warm water and used a sea sponge she'd given him to remove all traces of the salt scrub. He smelled like a large, aromatic-but-manly grapefruit and tingled from head to toe. This spa stuff wasn't bad, was it?

What *was* bad was his urge to see the delectable red-headed Peggy again, preferably naked. And he wished it would go away, seeing as how he wanted to kick her and her business partners off his property...and she probably wouldn't take kindly to that. Go figure.

Troy turned off the water and buried his face in a soft, clean towel. He rubbed at his hair with it, then dried his body and wound the towel around his waist. He stepped into some rubber shower thongs provided by the spa and reminded himself of his mission: to snoop. To make notes. To remember each and every detail of the place so that when he combed through the hundreds of pages of records and regulations, he could find something—anything—to nail them with and therefore break the lease.

He did feel regret about Peggy and her magic hands and her sweet smile with the single dimple. But when it came right down to it, this was just business, nothing personal.

PEGGY TOOK A COFFEE BREAK and watched wryly as one of Alejandro's pedicure clients, Monica Delgado, deliberately messed up the polish on one of her feet so that he'd have to redo it, and therefore spend more time with her. Monica liked to wear miniskirts for these occasions and flash the poor guy as much as she could. Today she also wore an array of toe rings: three different ones, set in white gold with expensive stones.

Alejandro's shoulders tensed as she called him back to the pedicure station, "embarrassed" by her clumsiness. But he smiled and joked with her, saying that Monica just enjoyed having him at her feet.

In the manicure area, the group of fortysomething ladies they'd dubbed The Fabulous Four gossiped and shrieked with laughter over what was probably their third bottle of wine. The downside to serving alcohol in the salon was that certain clients took total advantage of it. The Fab Four showed up like clockwork once a week, all at the same time, and indulged in a raucous happy hour at After Hours' expense.

But since they collectively spent so much money, Alejandro had decided that as long as they weren't allowed to drive drunk, the few bottles of wine and the noise were worth it. Today, the poor guy looked as though he should have a glass himself and maybe lie down on her massage table for a half hour.

There were days when After Hours was more zoo than spa. At his hairstyling station, one of the master cutters, Nicky, shrilly accused Sylvia of swiping a pair of his shears to cut her own bangs. She denied it at the top of her lungs.

Ugh. As the manager, it was Peggy's job to go break up the argument, calm them down and find the missing scissors. They turned up under the *GQ* magazine by his hand mirror, but when Peg suggested that he apologize to Sylvia, he sniffed and said he didn't like her attitude and she could kiss his left ass cheek.

Peg sighed, while Nicky launched into a long dialogue about how he couldn't find the right *man* to do it, no matter how many Internet dates he went on....

She finally took Sylvia into the back and explained that Nicky was experiencing a bad case of PMS and he'd be over it next week. Sylvia rolled her eyes and went to take her next facial appointment.

Peggy shook her head, took a deep breath and went back to the front of the salon, where she opened a tip envelope and stared at the enormous bonus Troy Barrington had left for her. Shirlie and Marly stared, too.

"That's, like, a thirty percent tip!" Shirl exclaimed.

Marly lifted a dark, winged brow, her expression teasing. "Sea salt scrub, hmm? You must not have missed an inch."

"Hey! Just what are you implying?" Peggy could feel her face flushing, though she knew her friends were just kidding around. "I do *not* finish off the clientele sexually, okay?"

"Maybe he wants you to think about it for next time," Shirlie said, with an evil wink.

Peggy drew herself up to her full height, which wasn't much taller than the receptionist sitting down. "There won't be a next time, ladies. Margaret can do the honors when he returns for his next treatment."

"I take it his happy-package was disappointing?" Shirlie probed for the information dear to her heart.

"Did I say that?" Peggy asked.

"Well, it *must* be tiny if you don't want to do him next time."

Peggy shrugged. She wanted to do him, all right. She just didn't think it was healthy for her to be around Troy Barrington in such an intimate setting— not until she'd purged the sexual attraction from her mind and body.

This is my year of self-discovery, she told herself firmly. *The year of Peggy Power. I'm not going to cater to anyone else, especially not a man. I'm not going to try to fix anyone's ego or gambling habit. I'm going to recover who I am and figure out how I got so out of balance last year.*

"Girls, I hate to disappoint you, but the size of Mr. Barrington's tip probably has more to do with the fact that I coach his nieces' powder-puff football team. He was just being nice."

The phone rang, forcing Shirlie to answer it. Peggy escaped to the kitchenette, where she found Alejandro looking elegant and tailored as usual, despite his recent harrowing experience with Monica Delgado. He was frowning and poking at something in the microwave.

"This tamal is still frozen," he explained. "And I am starving." She loved his slightly accented English—he was half Peruvian.

"They say patience is a virtue, doll."

He laughed. "How would *you* know, eh?"

Peggy stuck her tongue out at him. "I don't. But my New Year's resolution had to do with patience and impulse control."

"I can tell you're sticking with that," Alejandro said, "since it took you five seconds to make up your mind to move down here after I suggested the partnership."

She winced. Yeah, and it had taken her three seconds to decide what college to attend, two seconds to get engaged to a dud and one to buy a car.

He took pity on her by changing the subject. "So is

Hal still dating that crazy image consultant, up there in Connecticut?"

Peggy brightened. "Yes! As a matter of fact, they've moved in together. Can you believe that? A woman brave enough to actually live with my brother. And she's got him dressed like an actual human being now, and keeps his hair cut."

"Wonders will never cease." The microwave pinged, and he removed the tamal once again. This time steam rolled off it in waves, and the aroma of corn, garlic, onion and shredded pork was delicious.

Peggy watched Alejandro spread a huge quantity of Ahi (an unbelievably hot pepper sauce) over his tamal and dig in. How did the guy eat pure fire?

"Don't you at least want a glass of ice water?" She asked. "You know, for when your throat goes up in flames?"

He grinned and shook his head.

She opened the refrigerator and pulled out the lentil salad she'd made as part of her new, healthy, Peggy-Power regimen. She was not going to snarf fast-food pizza and burgers any longer. She was going to eat fiber and vitamins and leafy green vegetables. She was going to feel like a million bucks each and every day. Her chest swelled with pride as she mounded the lentils on a plate and sprinkled a few sliced green onions on top.

Shirlie walked in with a Wendy's Old Fashioned Hamburgers bag smelling of heavenly grease. "I super-sized my fries. Want some?"

Typically, it took Peggy half a second to decide. "Slap 'em right here," she said. "Where's the ketchup?"

SINCE THEY WORKED at the spa all day Saturday, Sunday was relaxation day, and Monday usually got taken up by errands and housework.

Marly was working too much to pay attention to her dating life, so she and Peg spent a lot of time together, this Sunday being no exception.

Peggy had sold everything she owned in a whirlwind garage sale before she'd driven to Miami from Connecticut. As part of her self-improvement program, she'd even sold her television, intending to read in her spare time instead of being sucked into sitcoms. Now she missed the TV's comforting presence, and she had an idea.

"You want me to *paint* a television on your livingroom wall?" Marly said incredulously.

"Yup. C'mon, you could do it in an hour with one hand tied behind your back."

"Yeah, but it's a nutty thing to do."

"It'll make the room seem more homey." Anything would make the sterile white box of an apartment seem more homey, even a fire extinguisher and a can of bug spray. It was awful. White tile. Beige carpet. White walls. White ceiling. White vertical blinds. She was living in a freakin' hospital. Every morning, she half expected to wake up in surgery.

"Uh, Peg?" said Marly. "The TV will have only one, unchanging image."

"I know! It's motion picture subversion. How cool is that?"

"Huh?" Marly started to laugh.

"Simplifying the constant barrage of images into one. But it'll be hard to choose which one I want."

"What's gonna be hard is convincing your landlord to give you back your deposit money."

Peggy waved that mundane thought away. "I'll just roll the walls white again before I leave. Can you do the TV today?"

"Sure, Miss Crazy. Bring me a pencil and think about what colors you want. Should I put it on that big wall over the couch?"

"Perfect. And I have some tempera poster paint. Will that work?"

Marly nodded, resigned to the project. She stood on the couch and lightly outlined a huge television screen on the wall, using the side of a framed art poster as a straightedge. "So, is this a plasma TV, Peg?"

"Oh, definitely. Only top-of-the-line equipment for me. Don't you agree?"

"Uh-huh. Get me some paint and some paper cups to mix colors in, okay?" Marly worked quickly, somehow making the sketch look three-dimensional.

They threw a sheet over the couch, and within half an hour Marley was painting in the frame and asking Peg, who was daydreaming about the possibilities of Troy Barrington's backside, what image she wanted on the screen.

Without even thinking about it she said, "A football

player's backside in uniform. He's bent over, gripping the ball and ready to hike."

Marly set down her brush. "Peggy. You really want to look at a *butt* every time you walk into your living room?"

"Yup. If it's a nice male one in spandex, I sure do!"

"Have you been sniffing too many aromatherapy candles, honey?"

"Probably. Hey, when you're done let's have a glass of wine and give each other pedicures. I think your laundry's just about done." Peg went to check on it, transferred the wet load to the dryer and got her cheap little foot spa out of the cabinet over the washer.

She brought it into the main room and set it down on a clean towel. Then she filled a pitcher with warm water from the kitchen sink and poured it into the basin. She added bath salts and brought out other supplies.

Marly was deep in concentration now, sketching the seat of the player's pants, his socks, cleats and hands on the football. Peggy was impressed that she didn't have to work from a photograph to get the details, proportions and angles right.

"Why didn't you go to art school, Marly?" she asked.

"I did."

"But you do hair."

"You know the story about why I didn't graduate. My dad got sick. Besides, I love what I do for women every day. I get to be creative, I make them feel better, it pays well and I'm never between jobs for longer than a couple of hours. What more could I ask for?"

Peggy nodded.

"And I'm able to do my art on the side." Marly painted in the football, somehow giving it texture and dimension, too. The stitching appeared almost real.

As Peg looked at it, the familiar wash of conflicting emotions about football rolled through her. It represented both success and failure for her, strength and weakness, power and victimization.

A guy like Troy Barrington—great, there she went, thinking about *him* again—had been a natural to play on a high school team, then a college one and finally go pro. He'd been encouraged all the way.

But her experience had been different. Suddenly, when she'd gone out for the high school team, she was resented. She'd made it because she was so good, but all the guys had looked at her funny. She'd cost one of their friends a place on the team. She had long hair and breasts and odd plumbing. She was just different with a capital *D*.

Instead of the camaraderie that someone like Troy had with the team, she'd battled sexually aggressive glances and felt bad because she couldn't share the same locker room, causing no end of logistical problems.

But she'd stuck it out. She'd won everyone's respect, however grudging. She could kick a decent field goal, run like the wind and would tackle anything that moved. The problem was, admittedly, that her body weight didn't stack up to a six-foot, two-hundred-pound male's.

Still, by the end of her senior year, she'd been practically the team mascot, carried on their shoulders when they won the district championship with *her* field goal.

Peggy would always proudly carry that moment in her heart, no matter what had happened later when she'd fought her way onto her college team. Nobody could take the district win away from her, not even her father's absence from the stands at the crucial moment.

Impulse struck again. "Marly, you're going to kill me, but I promise you a deep-tissue massage if you'll change the image on the screen."

"You're right, I am going to kill you." Marly straightened and glared at Peg.

"Please can you paint over the man butt and put a kick-ass woman there, instead? She's triumphant. She just kicked a field goal that won a big game."

"Why do I have a feeling that this kick-ass woman should have long red hair?" Resigned, Marly was already whiting out the other picture. "Get me a hair dryer, will you? It'll speed us up. I'm not staying here all night."

"Even if I make whiskey sours?"

"Okay, I'm staying all night. But you have to give me dinner, too."

"Deal. You know I wouldn't ask you to do this if you weren't so fast and so good."

"Yes, you would." Marly aimed the hairdryer at the wet paint, since trying to white out the wet image had just made a nasty smear on the wall. "So, um, Peg? How's that impulse-control thing going? I can see you're making huge strides."

5

TROY WIPED THE SWEAT from his temple with the sleeve of his T-shirt and reflected that there were more fun ways to get this hot and dirty. Redheaded ways.

He cast the thought out of his mind and bit back a smile as Derek mirrored his movements. They'd pulled every rotten plank off the back porch of his house; Derek had helped him measure all the new planks; and Troy was in the process of repairing the structural beams underneath.

He'd had professionals come in and replace the sagging porch roof, making sure it was done to city code. He'd have done it himself, but he didn't want the damn thing flying off or peeling back during the next hurricane to torment South Florida.

He and Derek were filthy, mosquito-bitten and tired, but the kid radiated happiness and a somewhat disturbing hero-worship that Troy felt he didn't really deserve. But he loved the boy's companionship and the fact that he inspired him to be a better person with a better attitude toward life. Derek somehow relieved his cynicism about the world and brought a smile to his face.

"Want a beer?" He ruffled the kid's hair.

Derek's eyes widened. "For real?"

Troy quirked an eyebrow and climbed through the back door, a little more difficult without the benefit of a porch floor. He returned with two cans and tossed the one marked A&W to his nephew.

The look on Derek's face was priceless: half relieved and half disappointed. "I thought you meant—"

"Last time I checked, you were eleven, not twenty-one." Troy grinned. "You've got ten years before I throw a Budweiser or a Spaten your way."

"What's a Spaten?"

"A good German beer."

"Oh." Derek popped the top on his root beer and said, "I don't really know why anybody thinks real beer tastes good. I've tried it before when nobody was looking. It's *nasty.*"

"I'm so glad you feel that way." Troy popped the top on his own can and drank deeply. Water would be better in this heat, but he couldn't resist the cold, bitter foaminess pouring down his parched throat.

"Hey, Uncle Troy?"

"Hey, what?"

"I was wondering if—" Derek broke off and twisted the aluminum can in his hands 360 degrees. He looked at it fixedly. "Um."

"Come on, just say it."

"Well, I'm s'posed to wait till Mom asks you, but it's really hard. Would-you-consider-coaching-our-Pop-Warner-team-'cuz-Mister-Vargas-quit." He said the last few words so quickly that Troy could barely understand them. "Mrs. Vargas has to have an operation and he's gotta take care of her, so he had to."

Troy blinked. *Oh, gee. What a promotion. I'm gonna go from coaching college ball to peewee....*

He hesitated. *I'm not qualified. I know nothing about kids except how to practice making them.*

Then curvy little Peggy's face flashed into his mind. *But if that redheaded gal can coach the girls, then I can coach the boys.*

He gazed down at the freckled, upturned face of his nephew, so eager and so hopeful, and knew there wasn't any question of what his answer would be.

"I'm sorry to hear about Mr. Vargas's wife," he said. "We'll have to send her a get-well card."

Derek nodded, but waited with bated breath. Finally Troy took pity on him. "And yes, kiddo. I'll coach your Pop Warner team."

Derek whooped and pumped his small fist in the air. *"Yesssss!"*

Troy grinned and tried to remember back to his own Little League days, but couldn't dredge up much. He sent up a silent prayer to the big quarterback in the sky. Surely there was some kind of a coach-the-kids instruction manual out there on the Internet?

By sundown they'd laid all the new planks on the porch and secured them with screws. Troy ordered pizza for himself and Derek and then dropped the boy off with Samantha again, slipping him twenty bucks for his help.

Troy had the perfect excuse to see Peggy Underwood again Tuesday night. He'd go to Danni and

Laura's powder-puff practice, cheer them on and also gather some clues about how to handle a large group of kids himself.

Every muscle in his body ached after the day's sweaty workout, and he wished like hell he were seeing Peggy tonight, for that hot stone massage. God, did that sound good!

He frowned, though, as he headed for the shower. Peggy wouldn't be doing the hot stone massage—some woman named Margaret would do it, even though he'd asked for Peggy and been flexible in terms of scheduling. She'd been booked all week, according to the receptionist. No, sorry, Miss Underwood didn't have any openings early next week, either.

Miss Underwood, he thought, had engineered things this way. And that intrigued him. Why didn't she want him on her table again? She'd looked at his chest as if she wanted to lick it. Miss Underwood, that delectable redhead, was avoiding him. Well, not for long!

Troy wasn't used to women avoiding him. They usually went out of their way to find an excuse to call him or see him again. And these were women with whom he didn't have anything in common, like football and a relationship with his nieces and admiration for Dan Marino.

On Tuesday he drove the Lotus to the practice field, where it wasn't hard to spot twenty-seven prepubescent girls running around in pink jerseys.

Peggy wore a faded pink T-shirt that hung loosely over her breasts and gray athletic shorts, her hair pulled into a ponytail and then threaded through a white baseball cap. Her muscular legs were covered with ginger freckles and her small feet laced into top-of-the-line cross-trainers.

"Hi, Peggy," he said, the sight of her making him feel like a horny caveman. Hmm, that ponytail was the perfect instrument for dragging the woman off to his cave and having his wicked way with her. *Here, ugg, ugg. Let me show you my big club....*

She whirled and stared at him, her expression unreadable behind mirrored sunglasses. Her lips parted. "Hi." She tugged at the brim of her hat and crossed her legs one behind the other, as if self-conscious about them. "I didn't, um, expect to see you here."

He smiled at her. "Oh, I just wanted to check on the twins. See you gals in action."

Danni spied him then, and came rushing over. "Uncle Troy!" She launched herself at him and gave him a bear hug, hitting him in the solar plexus.

"Oooof. Hey, Danni-girl! How ya doing?" She smelled of laundry detergent and grass and sunshine. So did Laura, who almost tripped over the last tire in the agility exercise and sprinted over to hug him, too.

His sister Samantha wasn't there; they'd come with an after-school carpool. But several mommy heads turned, sending admiring glances his way.

"This is our uncle," said Laura to Peggy. "He used to play for the Jacksonville Jaguars, and he's going to be coaching our punk little brother's Pop Warner team." Laura's eyes narrowed accusingly as she said this. "How come you're not coaching *us?*"

Whew, nothing like a little sibling rivalry to make things uncomfortable. Troy said calmly, "Because you already have a great coach in Miss Underwood, and Mr. Vargas needs someone to step in for him."

Peggy handled things beautifully. She winked at the girls. "Really," she mock-whispered behind her hand, "it's because your brother and the boys need the professional help. You girls are at the top of your game."

Danni laughed. "Yeah, the boys are pretty lame. I can kick a longer field goal than Derek can, and he knows it."

Troy didn't like the fact that she was right, since most of the girls were more developed at this age than the boys. His competitive streak reared its ugly head. *I'll be changing that, ladies. You can bet on it.*

Peggy nodded. "Okay, girls, get back out on the field. I need two more laps from each of you, and then we'll practice tackling and blocking before we play."

"Yes, ma'am." And the twins were off and running, leaving Troy and Peggy by themselves.

"So, you're awfully booked up for the next two weeks at the spa," he said casually.

She pressed a button on the stopwatch she wore on a cord around her neck and then turned to face him with a passable imitation of sincere regret. "I know, isn't it crazy? Everyone and her dog coming in for seaweed wraps and cellulite treatments." She shrugged as if to say, "What're you gonna do?"

"Bathing suit season approaches," he offered. Hmm, the thought of Peggy in a swimsuit was intriguing....

"Exactly." Her attention diverted again to the field,

she yelled, "Pick up the pace, ladies! Sprint into the homestretch!"

"So, do you go back to the spa after this?"

"Get those knees up, girls! I want to see them almost to your chests!" Peggy turned back to him and nodded. "Yeah. I just arrange to take two hours off in the afternoons on Tuesday, Thursday and Saturday. We schedule around it and Margaret picks up those appointments."

"So is Margaret as cute as you?" Troy asked, deliberately baiting her.

She turned to face him, and he saw his own smirk doubled in her mirrored sunglasses. "Now, how am I supposed to answer that?"

His smile widened. "Truthfully."

Her attention went back to the field. "Okay, walk and stretch!" Then she said to him, "Margaret is a very capable and skilled massage therapist."

Troy chuckled. "Yeah? Good to know, but that's not what I asked."

Peggy said stiffly, "She's very, uh, cute. In a manly sort of way."

Alarm bells went off in Troy's head. "What, does this woman have a beard? Hairy knuckles?"

"No! And by the way, your question is not appropriate. We hire people based on their qualifications, not their looks."

"Well, here's the thing," Troy said. "I don't think that this Margaret person could possibly be as qualified as you, Peggy. And as the customer, I demand top-notch service."

She lowered her sunglasses and aimed a level look at him. "What kind of game are you playing, Barrington?"

"Game?"

"Margaret actually has two years' more experience than I do, and I think you'll be very happy with her services. Now, I'm sorry, but will you excuse me?" She nodded politely at him and then jogged out onto the field, blowing an earsplitting whistle and gesturing to gather the girls around her.

Troy folded his arms across his chest and admired her rear view as well as her cool. He *really* was starting to wonder what flavor her freckles were.

THE SALON WAS LESS CROWDED this evening without the Fab Four, but just as wacky.

"Carnations!" Nicky hissed into his cell phone. Not for the first time, Peg thought he looked like Princess Di in drag—with much louder taste. Today he wore formfitting black overalls with a teal muscle T and a wide black leather cuff on his wrist.

"Yes, the tasteless little cheapskate sent me carnations…. Can you believe it? And I took him to a nice place, too!" Nicky stamped his foot, which was expensively shod in Italian leather.

"Well, what other dating sites are out there for us? Wait, let me get a pen…."

Peg tuned him out and went up to the front desk, where she was greeted with the unwelcome news that Margaret had gone home sick.

"You can't be serious!" Peggy stared at Shirlie and

groaned. "Margaret is never sick. She can't be, and especially not today of all days!"

Shirlie shrugged. "She is. Left an hour ago. Food poisoning from that taco place she loves. Uh, used to love. Her skin was as close to green as I've ever seen on a human being, and Alejandro had to drive her while she hung on to a wastebasket."

Poor thing.

"So you'll have to take her appointment this evening, and it's Troy Barrington."

Peggy closed her eyes. Troy Barrington, naturally. The guy who had slipped naked into her subconscious every night since she'd met him. The guy whom she really couldn't go near again, especially nude under a sheet, or she didn't think she could be held responsible for her actions. "Listen, Shirlie—I can't do it."

The receptionist looked at the appointment book. "Yes, you can. You don't have anyone coming until Pilar Morales at nine-fifteen."

"I, uh—"

The door opened and in walked Troy, with windblown hair and a slight sunburn on his nose. He looked edible, and those weird butterflies swarmed into her stomach again. She couldn't chalk them up to hunger this time. No matter how hard she fought against it, she was attracted to a *football player,* a species of man she'd sworn never to allow into her life.

"Hi," said Shirlie brightly, while Peg aimed a tight smile in his direction. "I'm afraid Margaret has gone home sick, so Peggy will be doing your hot stone treatment."

A devilish glint entered his eyes. "Is that so?"

Peggy cleared her throat and shot a Death Stare at Shirl, promising to get her later. "Ah, yes. I had a last-minute cancellation. How are you, Mr. Barrington?"

"Even better than when I saw you two hours ago on the practice field, Miss Underwood." He managed to say her name as if it were code for something deliciously dirty.

Underneath the pristine white lab coat, Peg's body went nuts, thrilling to every ion of his presence. The vibrations of his voice even played at the base of her spine.

He turned to Shirlie and gestured with his thumb at Peg. "She's got great legs, doesn't she?"

"Absolutely!" While Peggy turned red, Shirlie picked up the ringing phone and smiled. "After Hours, may I help you?"

You've been no help to me at all, thought Peggy darkly. *And what happened to your nervous babbling? Of all the times to be perky and quick-thinking...*

"So," said Troy, looking at his watch. "Massage, right?"

"Right. Follow me to the treatment room," said Peggy in wooden tones. *Barrington thinks I have great legs?* A shiver of pleasure went through her, even as she told herself not to be gullible.

"I think I'd follow you pretty much anywhere," Troy said, "because the view is so nice."

Should she ignore him or get in his face about the personal comments? She damn sure wasn't going to giggle and say thank you. Peggy settled for snorting. "God, and here I thought I'd left the cheese in the refrigerator."

"I guess I should be happy you're not calling me a dumb cracker."

She groaned. "He walks, he talks, he makes bad puns. Lord help me, what do I do with him?"

"Personally, I think you should go out on a date with him," Troy announced, whipping off his shirt. "If he asks you."

Peggy froze and then noticed what he'd done. "Whoa, whoa, whoa. Can you please keep the clothes on until I leave?"

"That's no fun at all."

"And I don't date clients." *I especially don't date football players.*

"Ah. Good thing the client hasn't asked you to date him yet."

Peggy choked. "Good thing."

"So, same drill, right? I shower, towel off, hang my robe on the hook, cover up Mr. Happy?"

She nodded and backed out of the room, feeling utterly discombobulated. Barrington was a big flirt. Problem was, she really wanted to flirt back. And it was *ever* so bad an idea. Her own personal goals aside, there were a hundred reasons not to ride the Troy Barrington roller coaster.

Peggy went to the kitchenette and got a glass of water for him and a glass of cold Arizona green tea for herself. She gulped some down and then pressed her chilled hands against her hot cheeks.

Inner calm. Balance. Mind, body and spirit in harmony. She took a deep breath and then exhaled; she repeated this three times. Then she walked down the hallway toward the treatment room as if going to her doom.

Troy was lying on his back, his arms folded under his head, his eyes open and amused. He flashed very white teeth as she entered the room again, his gaze following her every move.

"Water?" she asked him, adjusting the volume on the stereo. She had put on another soft, new age CD that was all instrumental.

"Thank you." He sat up, swung his legs over the side of the table and accepted the glass from her. She looked anywhere and everywhere in the room except at his broad shoulders and sleek, muscled chest.

Why had Margaret had to get food poisoning on this particular day?

She took a sip of her tea, set it down and then drew a rolling side table closer to him. He emitted some kind of aura, a force like a magnet. She could feel it, and instinct told her to go no closer.

Unfortunately her job required her to go closer to Troy, touch him, slide her fingers across his warm, damp skin and gently knead his flesh. But somehow she knew that if she did, there would be no turning back.

Peggy had dealt with creep clients and their pickup lines before. She'd sidestepped unwelcome advances and had no problem whatsoever refusing to work on someone who made her personally uncomfortable.

But the discomfort she felt around Troy wasn't due to any creepiness on his part…it was all about her primal response to him, the way he sprawled there with the sheet draped casually across his lap—and those seawater eyes inviting her to come sit in that lap.

She found her voice and was amazed that it sounded normal. "Want to get started? Why don't you lie down on your stomach?"

Troy shook his head. "No, I'll lie on my back. I want to watch you while you work."

Great. Just great. "All right."

He swung his powerful legs back onto the table, careless of the sheet that slipped dangerously low on his hips.

Peggy's mouth went dry as her gaze flew automatically to a dusky crevice exposed by the movement, and she jerked the sheet over him before her brain could even process what she'd seen. Dark curls and thickness. He was well-endowed in the diameter department, that was certain.

She stood next to him and looked down at him as he lay prone, memorizing the little details of his human terrain. The swells and valleys, the faint creases in his neck, his perfectly formed nose and lips. His eyebrows grew a bit wild, which only added to his manly appeal.

He raised an arm a little as if he wanted to curve it around her, but then stopped. If he hadn't, then nothing further would have happened between them.

But he did stop, seeming to remind himself that it was she who'd do the touching; that anything else was inappropriate and out of the question. He flattened his hand on the sheet and waited.

Peggy scooped massage cream out of a jar and

warmed it in her hands before putting them on his shoulders and applying it in *effleurage,* the term for the gentle stroking that initiated a body treatment.

Troy closed his eyes briefly and sucked in a breath. Then he opened them and stared into hers. Her hands stopped without her even realizing it. Abruptly she began again.

She wanted Troy to touch her. She'd never, ever wanted a client to do that. But he was different. His skin was hot beneath her fingers, his breathing as shallow and quick as her own.

No matter how she tried to tell herself that this massage was like any other, nothing personal, just business—it was a lie. She poured herself into this treatment as if she were making love to him, slowly, thoroughly and deeply.

She rubbed oil into each of his arms, silently stunned at the hardness of the muscle, the ropiness of the veins that stood out in clear relief against them. Steroids? She still wondered. Or just an intense daily workout for years upon years of playing football, basically from the time he could walk?

He wasn't puffy and bulky the way Eddie had been, especially toward the end when she'd left. Troy was hard and solid but streamlined. He looked like a man of endurance, patience and intensity.

How could just a single arm turn her on like this? But Peggy felt her breasts grow heavy and insistent against the cups of her bra. A trickle of perspiration ran down the small of her back, even though it wasn't hot in the room.

She reached Troy's wrist and then his hand, working the oil into his palm and wrapping her hand around each of his fingers in a warm, pulsing cocoon. She dipped into the valleys between his fingers, too, and the contact between them grew more intimate without a word or a move on his part.

It was just that she could sense his response, long before he curved his hand around hers and then interwove his fingers with her own, riveting her with his eyes while he did so.

Peggy froze, and after a moment he slipped his hand from hers.

"I'm sorry," he said softly. "I didn't mean to do that. It just…came naturally."

She nodded without speaking and moved to the other arm, smoothing the oil down it in one long motion. His skin glistened with it under the light, glowing like temptation itself. She traced one of his visible veins from elbow to wrist and tried to break the mood with conversation.

"You work out a lot." She said it as a fact, not a question.

He nodded, then reached up and laid a finger across her lips, whisper-soft.

She could have gotten angry—after all, who was he to give her orders, even if they were nonverbal? But she understood perfectly, and when he traced her bottom lip with that same finger, she felt the sensation at her core.

Slowly, not believing she was doing it, she took his index finger into her mouth and sucked the tip of it while he exhaled, his eyes riveted to the sight.

Mind, body, spirit. Impulse control.

But she knew sleeping with this man was inevitable. Her body didn't give a rip about her mind or her spirit right now—it had taken over. To hell with impulse control!

She moved her hands to his chest and lightly rubbed her thumbs over his nipples while his pupils widened in shock. She swept her hands over him, raking over his rib cage and following the indentations of muscle at his abdomen. She spread her fingers over his lower belly, diving slightly under the sheet and tickling the strip of hair that led down, down, down.

Troy tensed, pulled his finger from her mouth and clenched his own hands into fists. He waited to see what she would do, and she waited to see what he would do.

He was fully erect now, straining at the sheet. She struggled with the ethics of the situation. But hadn't she already thrown ethics to the winds?

Peggy closed her eyes and tried to resist this particular impulse of hers. It was dangerous and it was a form of self-betrayal.

But Hot Sex Personified lay on her massage table in front of her, ready, willing and clearly able. And she hadn't had any in so long. Instead, she'd had a dysfunctional relationship with a dysfunctional man, and she still wasn't sure why she'd stayed in it.

When she opened her eyes, Troy's gaze burned into hers, hot and amused and challenging on the most primal level. *Do me,* it said. *I'll make you scream.*

She was wet, and he knew it, and she knew he knew it.

She grasped the sheet, the cool white cotton against her heated skin. Should she remove it...or not?

6

HAD SHE LOST her mind? Peggy dropped the sheet as if it were scalding and backed away. "No," she said out loud. "I cannot be doing this, and especially not here."

On the table, Troy closed his eyes. "Okay. I can respect that," he said, then grinned. "But I sure don't have to like it."

She stared at him with something like despair. "Do you have to be so reasonable and calm? Why can't you be a total jerk and call me a cock tease or something? Give me an excuse to kick you out of here?"

Troy sat up again, propping himself up on his elbows, and smiled at her. "Do you want me to leave, Peggy?"

She swallowed. "No."

"Do you want me to stay?"

"No."

He laughed and swung his legs over the side of the table again, dangling them with his knees apart. Thank God the sheet was still in place. "What *do* you want? C'mere, babe."

She shouldn't have gone anywhere near him. But his eyes drew her, moth to flame. He grasped her hands and pulled her to within six inches of his chest, so that she stood intimately between his knees. They touched her hips.

She could smell the faint musk of his skin, see every bit of stubble on his face, the slight circles under his eyes and the laugh lines at the outside corners. He had heavy, lazy lids and lashes any woman would kill for. His jaw stretched wide and stubborn, his nose curved, slightly Roman, and his lips… God, those lips. They were parting, tilting and coming toward hers.

They took her mouth gently but firmly, not asking permission. He poured his desire into her and sought hers, licking it out from between her teeth and nipping it out of her lower lip. He sucked on her desire, pulling it from her until she gasped and tried to snatch it back, hide it again in all her secret places.

They wrestled over her attraction to him as if it were a live thing, but he finally took it hostage and she was forced to admit defeat—for the time being.

Satisfied, he relinquished her mouth, took her face between his big hands and dropped a kiss on her forehead. "It's gonna be okay, Peggy. It really is. Better than okay."

It was his kindness, his reassurance, his understanding that weakened her resolve again. He turned her hesitation into something charming instead of irritating and embraced it.

When he took her mouth again, the room seemed to drop away and she melted into him, conscious of nothing but his tongue stroking hers; his hands warm on her scalp, sifting through her hair; and the press of her breasts against his naked chest.

Soon his hands left her hair and he parted her lab coat, spanned her waist and then moved up to cup her breasts. The heat of him burned through her shirt and bra. She wanted desperately to feel his hands on her bare skin, and strained against them.

Troy tugged her blouse out of the waistband of her skirt and unbuttoned it, making a guttural noise of satisfaction when he discovered that she wore a front-clasp bra underneath. He made quick work of this, too, and her breasts were suddenly bare to his gaze, his hands and his mouth.

He held them with something close to reverence, rubbing his thumbs lightly over her nipples, and she almost came on the spot when he licked one and then finally, gloriously, fastened his mouth to it. She felt the pull of response at her sex, deep in her uterus and even in her veins as he triggered a flood of sensation with the one simple act.

Soon he'd moved to her other breast, and he squeezed them together, taking both peaks into his mouth. Her legs turned to rubber.

He pulled her against him so that she was caught between his powerful thighs and could feel his desire, pressing like a rock against her diaphragm. A series of sexual flashes tore through her, rogue electricity looking for an outlet.

Troy groaned softly, cupped her breasts in his palms and traced the inner rim of her ear with his tongue. His breath warmed and titillated the hundreds of tiny nerve endings there and seduced her utterly. She was his for the taking, and when he issued a command in the guise of a request, she obeyed.

"Lock the door, Peggy."

She stumbled back from him, her hair in her face. With one hand, he caught her upper arms to help her balance. With the other he tenderly tucked the renegade strands behind her ears. "You are so gorgeous."

She swallowed, caught her upper lip between her teeth, and somehow the door loomed in front of her without her being conscious of taking a single step. She saw her fingers turn the lock as if they were somebody else's, and then she was back against him.

Troy was standing now, naked and proudly, hugely erect. The sheet lay in disarray on the floor and he stepped on it as he turned her, slid his hands under her skirt. She felt his hands on her bare bottom, fingers sliding under the elastic of her panties, exploring her secret crevices. He brushed, featherlight, against her sex and she gasped for oxygen against his seeking mouth, hoping she hadn't robbed him of his breath.

He bit her lower lip gently and rucked her skirt up around her waist. Then he lifted her and set her down on her own massage table, legs spread to accommodate him. He snugged his heavy cock against her damp panties.

She pushed against it, feeling it twitch with urgency as Troy kissed her again, flattening her breasts against his naked chest.

He withdrew from her mouth and placed his hands on her thighs, thumbs inward. He flicked them up and down over her mons and drew teasing circles with one, then the other, around her clitoris.

Her breath coming in shallow gasps, she convulsed helplessly when he took a nipple into his mouth, too. Just as she quieted, he ripped her panties in two and slid the head of his penis against her. She came again instantly with glad shock, her eyes flying open as he drove deep into her. She clung to his shoulders for dear life, impaled, and his eyes seemed to pour into hers, drowning any trace of resistance she might have had left.

For a long moment he was content to simply rest that way, buried to the hilt in her. Then he moved, slowly and languorously pulling out, sliding in the slick honey of pleasure.

Troy's eyes went blind for a moment and then focused again on hers. "Condom," he groaned.

She didn't want him to go anywhere, do anything but what he was doing to her at that moment, but logic and responsibility prevailed. She swallowed and nodded. "I don't have one. Do you?"

He nodded, moving within her again. Then he kissed her and reluctantly pulled out. "Anybody in the locker room may be in for a rude shock," he said, his voice rough. Then he grabbed the spa robe off the hook on the back of the door and slung it around his body. He went off in pursuit of what they needed.

Peggy pulled the edges of her lab coat together and huddled on the massage table in the full knowledge that she'd lost her mind. What in the hell was she doing, having sex with a client on the job?

Troy didn't give her much time to think about it, though. He returned almost instantly. Seeing the look on her face and reading her body language easily, he took her clenched hands from her lap and kissed each white knuckle before unfolding them and giving her palms the same treatment.

His tongue slicked along her lifeline and told her exactly what his intentions were: pleasure and pleasure alone, no embarrassment or regret allowed. She melted into the moment, didn't resist when he spread the edges of her lab coat wide and slid her arms out of the sleeves, pushed her body back on the table and eased into the delta of her thighs once again.

She stared up at his chest and a ripple of a coming climax spiraled through her just at the sight. There was something about his sheer masculinity that melted her. She felt the pressure of his cock against her, seeking penetration. Shamelessly she lifted her bottom, spread her thighs until they ached and met the smooth, slick head of him. His blunt, thick penis sank into her and a streak of pleasure rippled through her to her midsection, eddying outward throughout her body.

She welcomed the sensual invasion and moved with him as he slid in and out. He toyed with her nipples as he set the rhythm, and nothing had ever felt quite so good.

A slow, liquid pressure built within her as she met him thrust for thrust, the root of him stimulating her outside while he stroked her inside as well. But what excited her most was his simple desire for her. She could read it in his touch and his gaze.

Footsteps and voices traveled through the hallway outside and kicked her former anxiety into play again, but Troy just grinned, laid a finger on her lips and pushed deeper, cupping her bottom to brace her.

"I'm gonna come, babe," he whispered. "It feels too good and I can't hold on anymore...."

She grabbed his butt and wrapped her legs around him until she could cross her ankles, holding on to him as if she'd never let go. A glow began to surface from some primal place within her, and it grew brighter and brighter.

Perhaps it was the possibility of discovery that sent them both flying over the precipice at the same moment. Troy opened his mouth in a silent curse, arched his back and impaled her in one sudden motion. She exploded with a cry that he smothered with his lips and echoed with a groan. They lay like that for a long moment, their hearts beating wildly against each other.

Oddly enough, it was the supposedly calming music that brought Peggy's anxiety back in a wave.

She felt pinned by his big body, and put her hands against his chest as if to push him off. He seemed to note the change in her mood immediately, and pulled out, his gaze assessing her face.

He picked up the sheet from the floor and wrapped it around his waist as she struggled up and pulled her skirt down again. She slid off table, and an awkward postcoital moment ensued as she snapped her bra back together and buttoned her blouse. What could she possibly say?

Thank you, Troy, for the three orgasms?

I'm really not this kind of girl?

So, do I tip you *thirty percent this time?*

She backed away from him, her heartbeat thudding in her ears. "Troy, I just want to say… I'm not a groupie. I'm not a bimbo."

"I know that," he said, putting on the spa robe and tying the belt.

"I shouldn't have done what I just did. I'm at my place of employment."

He moved toward her, gathered her hair in his hands and kissed her nose, of all things. "Will you have dinner with me later?"

Peggy froze. The sexual encounter was bad enough, but to actually follow up on it? Act as if this was all in a day's work? She licked her swollen, thoroughly kissed lips. "I don't date football players, not ever."

"Why not?"

Her three reasons were years in the past, but she wouldn't talk about them. Not to him, not to anybody. "I just don't."

"That's ridiculous." He crossed his arms over his chest and squinted down at her. "And a guy buying you dinner once doesn't mean you're dating him. Besides, as long as we're splitting hairs, you should keep in mind that I'm no longer a football player."

She stared at the floor and then her shoes, which were scuffed on the toes.

"Fine," he said. "It doesn't have to be dinner, just a drink. One. That's it. If you still feel the same way after that, I'll leave you alone."

She hesitated, then capitulated. "Okay."

"What time do you get off tonight?"

"Ten-thirty, after my last appointment."

"I'll pick you up then. I assume that you don't want to finish our session at the moment, since you're uncomfortable."

I want to finish it, all right. But not in any way that's decent or professional. "At this point, there simply isn't enough time—I have another appointment at 9:15. Do you mind rescheduling?"

"I don't care, as long as it's you who does the massage." And with a last kiss, Troy disappeared into the showers.

LATER, AS PEGGY CLEANED UP after Pilar Morales's seaweed wrap, she felt like a time bomb. A bomb in a too-tight bra, with no panties on. She'd buried the ripped ones in the trash long before Pilar had arrived.

She still couldn't quite believe that she'd allowed Troy Barrington to seduce her on the job! She could sterilize and disinfect the place to her heart's content, but her actions didn't change the facts.

It's been a year since Eddie, she told herself. *I have a right to a normal libido, especially when a man who looks like Troy comes on to me. Any other woman would have done the same thing....*

But it didn't square her conscience completely. She'd failed miserably at impulse control, yet again.

Peg finished work by throwing the sheets and towels into the wash. She tossed in some soap and started the machine, which made a groaning, churning noise—exactly the way she felt inside. If only she had a rinse cycle to filter out her emotions and fears.

Troy Barrington was probably waiting for her outside already, so they could go have that drink. But after she ditched her white lab coat and threw it into the machine, too, she grabbed her tote bag and ran for the bathroom. Peggy splashed cold water on her face, brushed her teeth and fixed her hair.

She cast a last dissatisfied look into the mirror, pinched her stupid pug nose in a futile attempt to make it narrower—why had he kissed it?—and slung the tote over her shoulder. She took a deep breath and marched out of the bathroom, hoping Shirlie would be gone.

She was, but Marly pounced on her before she could get out the door. "What's going on, Peggo? Troy Barrington left two hours ago, but he's now waiting for you outside."

Peggy became fascinated with the array of nail polishes on the wall behind Marly. "I'm, uh, going to have a drink with him."

Her coworker stared at her. "What happened to inner balance and a year alone and Peggy Power?"

"It's just a drink."

"Uh-huh." Marly smirked. "Then bottoms up, hon! But I want to hear all about it tomorrow."

"Just do me a favor, will you? Don't tell Shirlie."

"Shirl has a nose like a bloodhound. She'll sniff it out within seconds."

"Well, try to keep it from her as long as possible, okay? I think she has a crush on Troy."

Marly nodded.

"And it's just a drink."

"Right."

"It's not even dinner."

"I hear you."

"I coach his nieces, so we'll probably just talk about them and how I can help improve their game."

"Peggy, just shut up already and go meet the guy? He's right outside the door."

And he was. With her heart sitting on her tonsils, Peg opened it, walked out tentatively and said, "Hi."

He seemed amused. "Hi." Then he reached out and took her hand. "Do you want to go to a bar?"

"We could. Or we could just go to my place or yours and get this out of our systems."

7

TROY'S JAW DROPPED OPEN. This woman was nothing if not direct. "Get it out of our systems?"

"You know," Peggy said, "this lust thing. We both want to act on it. So we should just get it out of the way and move on, don't you agree?"

Troy stared at her. "No, I don't agree. I'd like to get to know you." The words surprised him as much as they seemed to surprise her.

She stared back at him, seeming perplexed, while he felt the same way. This obviously wasn't the answer she'd expected—and quite frankly it wasn't the answer he normally would have given. Wasn't no-strings-attached sex every guy's fantasy?

"But it's easier this way," she argued. "You don't have to struggle with the first, second, third and fourth down. You just score."

Troy said, "Where's the fun in that? It's like the opposite team handing you the ball and inviting you over the goal line. There's no game. That sucks."

"You didn't seem to object to scoring a couple of hours ago."

"I certainly did not, but that was a surprise outcome. I didn't expect that you'd—"

"Be that easy?"

"Don't put words in my mouth, Peggy. I don't think you were easy at all. I sensed there was a real struggle going on inside you. It made me want you even more."

"Oh, but now that I say I'm ready to jump you, you lose interest. See, it's all a game. A mind game."

"I'm not here to play a mind game, and who said I've lost interest? You're being extremely difficult. In fact, most guys would take off at this point."

"No, they wouldn't." Peggy stuck out her chin. "Most guys would take me up on the invitation to my apartment."

He blew out an exasperated breath. "Okay, you have a point," he conceded. "But consider the possibility that I might see more in you than a one-night stand, okay?"

Her eyes flashed provocatively. "What if I don't see the same potential in you?"

Troy stopped and pulled her to him so that their bodies touched. He felt her heartbeat accelerate and smiled. "Then I'll just have to change your mind, won't I?" He angled his head toward hers and noted that she raised her mouth for his kiss. Instead of delivering on her expectations, he left her wanting and walked in silence to his car, where he opened the door and turned to hand her in.

She'd stopped, and now she stared from the car to him. She put a hand over her mouth. "You're the *stalker!*" She backed away.

Oh, hell. Not this.

"I recognize the car now. I couldn't figure out why you looked familiar...."

"I'm *not* a stalker. I was sitting in the parking lot because I'd just come out of Benito's," he lied. "And I got a call on my cell phone. Then I saw you notice me, and I was afraid you'd think just what you thought. So I ducked down."

"Why am I not believing this?"

"Because you have a suspicious nature?" He stared her straight in the eye. "Look, if I were some kind of perverted creep, don't you think I'd have been more aggressive with you before?"

She chewed her lip. "Well, I did make it pretty easy for you."

Troy sighed. "Fine. I'm a weirdo and a stalker. I have piano wire, a shovel and a bag of cement in the trunk." He popped it for her, and she could see that there was nothing there.

"Why did you leave when I told you I'd called the cops?"

"Because I really didn't want to get into a conversation with them, or be written up for something I wasn't doing!"

"Oh."

"Would you like to have that drink now?" He patted the door. "The salon has my name and number, remember."

She clearly felt foolish now, but still she struggled for the upper hand, like the scrapper she was. "You don't have to do that," she told him, finally getting in. "Open doors and put on the gentleman show for me."

It's just a stalker thing, honey. She didn't know it yet, but she was going to lose. "I want to do it. And it's not a show." Troy shut the door and walked around the front of the Lotus.

He opened the driver's-side door and slid in next to her. Peggy's hair smelled sweet, like jasmine and honey—in marked contrast to her sharp, cynical words. It was yet another contradiction about her that intrigued him.

"Okay, so now that we've established that I'm not a stalker," he said, "why are you trying to sabotage this thing between us before it even gets off the ground?"

"Hey, I'm just trying to cut through the dating bullshit, you know? I'm so sick of it."

He shook his head at her. "The 'dating bullshit,' as you call it, can be fertilizer. Something extraordinary might bloom from spreading it around."

She laughed. "You have a refreshing perspective on all this, don't you, Troy?"

"Your own perspective is certainly unique—though I won't call it refreshing. I call it downright cynical."

"C'mon, I'm just brave enough to verbalize what we're all thinking. How many times have you sat opposite a woman and thought, *Christ. I already know I can't stand her but I have to sit through two more hours of this and then pay for her dinner and drive her ass home.*"

Troy couldn't help but laugh.

Peggy continued in a parody of a man's voice, "And I probably won't even get a good-night kiss for my trouble, much less get laid."

This went so far as to get a pig snort out of him while he tried to catch his breath. Finally he said, "You are not a nice woman."

"I agree. But am I accurate?"

"Maybe."

"So why don't we have that drink at either your place or mine and not play the games?"

"All right, all right. We'll go to yours. Mine is a wreck, since I'm in the middle of remodeling."

"Great. Take a left up here, and then an immediate right.... By the way, I'm not a slut. It's just that you're... different."

He hooted. "If I only had a nickel for every time I've heard *that* line from a woman."

Peggy seemed nonplussed.

"What, no caustic comment? As long as we're being up-front and not playing games, darlin', I'm fully aware that it was my wallet and my job that were 'different,' not me." *But those days are gone,* Troy thought gloomily. *Now I'm chopped liver.*

"I'm not impressed by money," she said stiffly. "And I'm not impressed by your former football stardom, either. I made my college team and started, too."

Silence fell in the car.

"You *what?*" Troy asked. "Was it a women's college?"

"No," she said icily, "it was not. It was Bryce University."

After a stunned moment he said slowly, "I remember reading about it. How a girl fought her way onto the team, a placekicker. That was *you?*"

"That was me."

He looked at her with new respect. "I'll be damned. What was it like for you? To be the only woman in that sea of testosterone?"

She avoided his eyes. "Let's just say that I had my highest highs and my lowest lows during the season I played."

"Why didn't you go back?" Troy pulled the Lotus into the parking lot behind an apartment building. He was pretty sure he already knew the answer to that question. The guys would have made it miserable for her, and even male placekickers weren't viewed with respect. They weren't considered "real" players, didn't go through the same drills or practice plays.

She avoided the question by getting out of the car before he'd cut the engine, not waiting for him to open her door. Her hair fell down her back like a coppery waterfall, ending just above a neat little waist and a spectacular ass. Those legs were solid with muscle, only the inner thighs soft and welcoming.

Troy liked the way the moonlight softened her, bathed her in a gentle glow. He tried to divert himself from the thought that she was bare to the air under her black cotton miniskirt. He'd ripped the panties off her, after all. She couldn't possibly have salvaged them.

Peggy tossed him an impatient glance over her shoulder, unaware that despite his words about getting to know her he'd have loved nothing better than to bend her over the hood of the Lotus, soft and willing and even begging for the release he could bring her.

He groaned inwardly as he imagined her spread-eagled on the car, lush breasts flattened against the warm metal, hair tumbled over her naked back and that sweet ass, among other things, bare to his gaze. He'd wanted to do all kinds of dirty things with her, ever since he'd seen her from the parking lot that first night.

Obviously, something about her just brought out the pervert, if not the stalker, in him. He'd better get a handle on his fantasies.

He caught up with her in three long strides and reminded himself that he couldn't get involved with this girl. What was he thinking? Hadn't he been delivered a four-inch stack of city regulations? Didn't he, right at this very moment, have notes in his pocket on possible violations After Hours had committed?

He felt sleazy. *Yeah, you're some gentleman, big guy. No doubt! You seduce her on her own massage table while you're planning to kick her off the premises. Nice.*

But he fixated on her miniskirt again. He wanted to chew it off like a goat.

PEGGY UNLOCKED her apartment door with difficulty, since Troy's mouth was doing incredibly sexy things to the back of her neck and her ears, while his hands were unashamedly roaming over her breasts, peeling back her bra to cup them and teasing her nipples exquisitely.

In fact, he flattened her body against the door, pinning it with his while his cock nudged the cleft of her buttocks through the thin skirt she wore. He was seeking entry much as she sought the lock with her key.

"The neighbors," she whispered, feeling his fingers lift her hem. She managed to turn the key, and they almost fell through the door to the beige carpet inside.

Troy kicked the door closed, turned her in his arms and tossed her handbag aside. He lifted her and set her on the seat of the fat, overstuffed sofa she'd bought secondhand. Then he dropped to his knees in front of her and slowly pushed her skirt up her thighs.

He bent his head and kissed each of her knees while she fell back against the pillows, her breathing fast and shallow. He spread her legs and gently, expertly touched his tongue to her, his breath warm and intimate and whispering over her heated flesh.

The sensation was indescribable, and she lost herself to it, their surroundings dropping away until nothing existed except for his mouth and her pleasure.

He slicked over her folds, separated them, licked into her until a thousand nerve endings screamed and begged for more. Any shyness she may have felt was lost to ecstasy and became unimportant.

Troy grabbed her bottom and tugged her forward as she squirmed with the intensity of it, unintelligible sounds finding their way out of her mouth. She was completely at his mercy and she knew it—didn't like it as an abstract concept, but adored it as a woman.

He left her outer folds to circle inward, closer and closer to her clitoris. And when he found it and sucked hard, she lost control, a cry ripping from her throat as she exploded in his mouth.

She tried to get away from the exquisite torture then,

but he gripped her firmly and kept teasing the nub with his tongue until she screamed again and utterly disintegrated into nothing but waves of delicious pleasure—pleasure so intense that it bordered on pain.

"Stop," she begged him, fisting her hands in his hair. "You have to stop."

Disbelief filled her as he left his mouth where it was, waiting for her to quiet before he initiated her desire yet again, with slow, patient, featherlike touches at the very edges of her sex. He bit and sucked at the innermost parts of her thighs, the curve of her cheeks. He blew on her clitoris, cooling it in the most erotic way possible. He didn't touch it, seeming to understand that would be too much.

He began her journey again by focusing on her outer labia, tickling and teasing until the rest of her developed a sensual envy. Exhausted, she arched her back and met him anyway, melted under his touch as he brought her to the peak of climax yet one more time.

Impossible, she realized, but she'd orgasmed three times without him inside her, and they were both still wearing their clothes. She wanted to feel the fullness of his cock, stretching her to capacity and stroking her where his tongue simply couldn't reach.

She stripped off his shirt—he didn't exactly protest—and unbuckled his belt. She unbuttoned his fly and shoved his jeans down his hips, freeing his engorged penis. As she took it into her hands he groaned, encouraging her to move her palms against the smooth skin and slide them up and down.

Somehow she wriggled out of her own clothes while he found a condom and rolled it on. She straddled him, rubbing herself against his shaft until he grabbed her hips, forcing them down while he thrust roughly upward. She gasped as he entered her, throwing back her head and experiencing slick, dark, powerful pleasure.

He set a fast tempo that excited her all over again, driving into her with a fierce possessiveness that was purely masculine, primal and urgent.

Troy pulled her shoulders down as he thrust, bringing her breasts within range of his mouth. His bristle scraped the aureoles of her left nipple, painful but erotic. Then it was in his mouth and he was sucking, pulling electricity through her hot spots again and filling her veins with a roar of heat.

He mastered the other breast and then rolled her under him, her wrists pinned over her head, while he thrust again and again. His face flushed dark and his eyes glazed with pleasure, he stole her lips again in a deep, intimate kiss. His tongue in her mouth echoed his cock between her legs, until finally he climaxed in a single mighty stroke and spilled himself inside her, moaning her name into her hair.

She ground herself against the root of him and his aftershocks set her off again, too, melting her in a rush of warm, sweet honey. She had a sinking feeling, as she floated back to the surface of reality, that Troy Barrington had ruined her for any other man.

8

THE NEXT DAY Troy stood in the baking afternoon heat and listened to Joe Vargas give him the rundown on Pop Warner football. The man's wedding ring gleamed in the sun, accentuating his wholesomeness and making Troy feel like even more of a drinkin', fornicatin' bottom-feeder.

He had been up all night having sex with a woman he needed to betray for his own ends. He was a complete shit-heel. What business did he have trying to be a role model for a group of kids?

Worse, he wanted to see Peggy again in the worst way. And he couldn't do that. He really, really couldn't.

"So the secret is," declared Joe, "you've got to find the fine line between tough and supportive. You can't push them too hard—they're only eleven years old. It's a lot more important at this stage that they learn good sportsmanship than that they win the game."

Troy nodded as if he were absorbing pearls of wisdom. Surely this was just common sense?

The kids on the field were scrimmaging in an enervated formation, wilting in an early burst of summer.

The air was hot, stagnant vapor without a single

breeze. It hung over them like a vast, wet cloth, smothering anyone who tried to suck oxygen from it.

Vargas had gone into the politics of the team, specifically what the parents were like and how that affected their children's attitudes and behavior. Troy tried to focus and retain what he said.

"Bobby Pitkin, now, his dad's a real problem. Wants his kid to be the star no matter what, even if another kid gets hurt. You gotta watch him and step carefully. On the other hand, Aaron Tate's parents don't want him playing football at all—it's his grandpa who signed him up. The father is a musician and worries about Aaron's hands...."

By the time the boys were through with their warm-up, Troy had the goods on everyone. He and Vargas took them through some simple running plays together, and then had them play a nine-on-nine game: shirts against skins.

In the middle of it, Bobby Pitkin's dad showed up, veering erratically in his red SUV, and climbed out to entertain himself by causing trouble. He started yelling instructions and other things from the sidelines, annoying the group of moms who sat in the bleachers.

Joe growled under his breath, "Guy's a prize jerk. Owns his own construction company and shows up here a lot after having a few Jack Daniels for lunch."

Troy listened to him for a while, his disgust growing. "I'm not putting up with that guy."

"Watch it. He's connected around town and he could cause trouble."

"I don't care." Troy strolled over to the man. "Hi, I hear you're Bobby's father."

The man was clean shaven, dressed in pressed clothes, but sure enough, he stank of whiskey. "Who're you?"

"Troy Barrington. Used to coach the Jaguars. Now I'll be coaching this peewee team."

Pitkin ignored him for a moment, shouting onto the field, "Bobby, you pussy! Knock him down. Which part of the word *tackle* do you not get?" Then he turned back to Troy. "That's quite a demotion, buddy. Then again, the way the Jaguars been playin' for the past two seasons, any peewee team could beat 'em."

Troy made himself count to ten slowly so he wouldn't pound the guy's face into the ground. In the meantime Pitkin exercised some more of his natural charm.

"Run, you little prick!" he roared at Bobby. "Run! By God, you better get your hands on that ball, or I'll get my hands on *you*."

Troy decided that he'd had enough. He began politely, suggesting to Pitkin that it might be counter-productive to call Bobby a "pussy" and that this term was also offending the ladies present.

Frank Pitkin declined the advice, so as the new coach Troy slung an arm around his shoulders and walked him off the field without anyone else knowing for sure that it was by force.

He didn't harm him in any way, just removed him. Like a true gentleman, he walked Frank to the door of his Toyota 4Runner and helped him into it, ignoring the man's insults and threats to have him fired before he'd even started.

"You want little Bobby to play on this team?" Troy

asked. "Then you don't verbally abuse him from the sidelines or make the atmosphere uncomfortable for the other parents. If that isn't clear enough, or you feel you need to challenge me on this, you can take it up in front of the school board."

Frank Pitkin suggested that Troy screw himself with a two-by-four, and instead of pounding the man's face into his steering wheel, Troy just nodded and said he'd take it under advisement.

Dadzilla sped away in a cloud of rage and dust.

Troy felt that perhaps he'd done something to redeem himself. He went to ask Joe Vargas who Bobby could get a ride home with.

The skins won the game, and after discussing with the shirts how they could have done things differently, Troy and Vargas talked to the boys about sportsmanship.

"The world of sports is competitive," Troy told them. "But you've got to make sure you don't let the competition turn you into a jerk. Winning is great, but it's attitude and playing the game that's most important. You don't call each other names, you don't cheat or injure other players to gain the upper hand. You don't walk around like a grouch. Got it? I don't care how many points you score, if you behave like that, you are a *loser.*"

He bought sodas for everyone and said he'd see them next time.

His mood stayed up until after he'd driven Derek back to Samantha's house and he sat at the scarred kitchen table in the Coral Gables shack, staring with distaste at a greasy fast-food burger.

He ate it because it was there and better than the alternative: three-day-old garlic beef and a leftover pork egg roll that had been fried in rancid peanut oil to begin with.

Troy rinsed off the chipped plate he'd put the burger on, and watched a parade of tiny sugar ants emerge from a corner of the kitchen window. If he hosed them down with bug spray, he'd just have to inhale the nasty stuff, and a new line of them would be back tomorrow.

He looked at the four-inch stack of city regulations governing building codes and permits that sat like an oversize brick on the sagging cushions of the former owner's olive-green couch. He sighed and hauled them into the room he planned to make his office, dropping the stack onto the computer table with a thud. He might have done a good thing today, but he still felt like an asshole. However, this was business. He needed that retail space. It didn't make any financial sense to pay rent somewhere else when he owned the building.

He armed himself with a Spaten and a Cohiba and got to work, looking specifically at electrical and plumbing code. He wouldn't be surprised if the business partners at After Hours had used illegal labor to cut costs on some of the installation. And if they'd cut corners that way, then it stood to reason that they might not have all the correct permits.

PEGGY SURPRISED EVERYONE, especially herself, by singing at work the next day. The singing wasn't particularly tuneful, and the lyrics weren't from anything hip, but just the fact that she warbled stanzas of actual song was a shock. "'I wanna hold your haaaaand…'"

"What's wrong with you?" Shirlie asked. "You sound happy, and you're never happy in the morning."

"Even Oscar emerges from his trash can occasionally," said Peggy, breezing by in a clean white lab coat.

"Now you're putting yourself on par with Muppets?"

Peg just smiled and disappeared into the back.

Marly was the next to comment, when they came nose to nose in the supply closet. "Just one drink, huh? What's with the circles under the eyes and the bow-legged gait?"

"So maybe it was a couple of drinks."

"Uh-huh. Are you going to see him again?"

Peggy shrugged and tried to look as unconcerned as possible. Unfortunately the intercom squawked next to her ear, and Shirl's voice said, "Peg? You have the most massive floral delivery here…. I swear it's an entire South American jungle. Birds of paradise, orchids, tiger lilies, nasturtium—there's a good possibility there's a leopard hiding in here somewhere. Can you come up and get it?"

Marly tagged along, and her eyes widened when she saw it. "God Almighty, if it's not the rest of the Amazonian rain forest!"

The arrangement was huge. Peggy stepped into the reception area just in time to see Shirlie holding the sealed card up to the light, trying to read the message and identify the sender.

"I'll take that, thanks."

"Who? Who? Who?" Shirl was almost jumping up and down.

Peg twitched the card out of her hand and unsealed it. The sender had written, "You are unforgettable. Looking forward to seeing you again."

She tried to sidestep the receptionist, but Shirlie must have leaped over the reception desk like Daisy Duke over the door of the General Lee. "Who are they from?"

A wide smile had taken over Peggy's face completely without her permission. *That's for me to know and you to find out?*

Shirlie, despite being a babbling bubblehead, caught on fast and let out a jealous shriek. "It's Troy Barrington, isn't it!"

So much for keeping a secret.

"Oh…my…God! He's such a dream! He sure must like your massages!"

Among other things. Peg's fair skin betrayed her: she felt herself blushing at some of the things she'd done last night. Maybe she *was* walking a little bowlegged. But at least she had panties on today.

Since Shirlie was looking at her with high suspicion, Peggy pulled the arrangement into her arms, staggering under its weight. She buried her face in it to avoid looking at her coworkers and inhaled the green, leafy scents.

The lilies and nasturtium had no smell, nor did the birds of paradise, but the orchids filled her nose with sweet heaven and mingled with the earthy, damp scent of moss and the dried grasses used to weave the basket container.

How long had it been since a guy had sent her flowers? She couldn't even remember the last time. A vague memory surfaced: on their first Valentine's Day together, Eddie had brought her a dozen roses wrapped in clear plastic and secured by a rubber band. They'd still had the grocery-store price sticker on them.

It wasn't that the roses weren't pretty. They were. But Eddie had just walked in with them, plunked them on the table of the apartment they shared and then said, "Hang on. I gotta fill this out first."

From inside his jacket he'd produced a dog-eared card which he filled out in front of her, scrawling "Happy V-Day, Love Eddie." Then he'd dug his pinky into his ear to scratch an itch before handing both card and flowers to her and shoving his hands into his pockets.

Peggy had never received an elaborate, expensive floral arrangement like this one, and in spite of her cynicism, she was charmed. A warm, mushy feeling spread through her stomach and stayed there until, unable to see over the plant life in her arms, she almost ran over Alejandro.

"Since when do I need a machete to hack my way through the hallway?" he asked. "Did someone die?"

"No," Peg said, craning her neck around a patch of orchids. "Someone likes me."

"Miracles will never cease," he declared. "Who has the poor judgment to do that?"

"Ha, ha." She made it into the kitchenette and set the flowers in the middle of the small table, leaving only about four inches around the edges for anyone's plate or cup.

"The salad course is served," said Alejandro.

I am unforgettable? Really? Peggy mooned over the flowers in a disgustingly girly way, feeling the goofy grin spreading across her face.

She did her best to wipe it off, but by the time she got down to work, she was floating on a silly pink cloud, humming as she gave Pugsy Malloy his weekly rubdown.

She watched her hands all but disappear into his squishy white flesh and for the first time it didn't really bother her. She kneaded him as if he were dough, worked him on the table until he gasped like a dying fish, wiped away the perspiration that rolled off him without a blink.

Pugsy disappeared into the showers a happy man, while Peggy fantasized every time the phone rang that it was Troy Barrington. When she caught herself doing it, she felt pathetic. Why didn't she take the initiative? After all, he'd sent her flowers. She should call him and say thank you.

She'd whipped out her cell phone to dial his number when she realized that she didn't know it. She'd have to get it out of the appointment book at the reception desk. Ugh.

"So has he asked you out?" Shirlie pried, before Peg could even ask her for the book.

No use pretending she didn't understand. "Um. We went for a couple of drinks last night."

"And?"

"Shirl, how are we stocked for highlighting foil?"

"Aha. You're avoiding the subject, which means Something Happened. So is he a good kisser?"

"Because I'm trying to get that order together. The rep will be by tomorrow—"

"We're fine. So about the kissing? Lots of tongue action? Little nibbles? Does he go for the ears?"

There simply was no explaining to Shirlie that she was Peg's friend but not her confessor—especially not of intimate personal details!

"Can I see the appointment book, please?"

"Why? I gave you the day's schedule. And you're holding out on me!"

"Shirlie, there's really nothing to tell," Peggy said firmly, and rounded the reception desk to grab the book. "I hate to disappoint you, but it was just a couple of drinks."

Shirlie pouted and chewed her Cupid's bow lip. "Well, what does he drink? I'm guessing bourbon. And what did you talk about? His glory days in pro ball, right?"

Peg silently counted to three and refrained from clobbering her with the appointment book. "He drank Tanqueray and tonic last night, but he usually sticks with beer. And we talked about the Marlins, actually, and his sister," Peggy fibbed as she flipped back a couple of pages in the book, found Troy's number and silently memorized it.

Once she'd gotten away from Shirlie, she closed the door of the wet room behind her and dialed. He answered on the third ring. "Hello?"

"Troy? It's Peggy."

He paused. "Hi, Peggy." Was it her imagination, or did his tone sound a little cool?

"I just wanted to thank you for the flowers—they're stunning."

"What flowers?"

Her mouth went dry. Then her entire body broke out in a sweat. And her heart dropped into her stomach. She opened her mouth, but no sound came out.

He chuckled, but it sounded forced, not genuine. "So you've got a secret admirer."

She finally forced her voice past her utter humiliation. "I guess so. Uh, I didn't mean to put you on the spot, but after last night I just assumed they were from you."

"I wish they were. I feel like a jerk now. I probably should have sent you some flowers."

"No, no...."

"But then you'd have a surplus, wouldn't you?"

She produced a half laugh.

A painful, awkward silence fell between them. Where was the camaraderie of last night? Peggy wanted to hang up and take a bath with her toaster oven. Her miserable life would be over then, and she could go right to hell.

Troy cleared his throat. He started to speak, caught himself. After a moment's hesitation, he said in a rush, "But if you're not tied up with your secret admirer, would you like to have dinner with me?"

"Uh, sure!"

"Great. That's great," he emphasized, as if it wasn't at all but he was making the best of it.

Oh, God, she thought. *He didn't mean it. He had no intention of asking me out, but he felt obligated to since I called him. He was being polite. I should have said no.*

Her face started throbbing with heat. The bath with the

toaster was looking better and better...maybe she'd throw in the hairdryer, too, just for a little added excitement.

She heard his voice rumbling through the phone but didn't register what he'd said. "Um, could you repeat that, please?"

"I asked what time I can pick you up."

"Right. Of course you did." *How about never?*

"Will you be at After Hours? Is nine too early?"

"Nine is fine." The words came out of her mouth before she could concentrate on a good lie, like she was booked until midnight for the next three years.

"Okay. We can just walk over to Benito's. I'll make a reservation."

Peggy wrapped her natural sarcasm around her like a protective blanket. *Fabulous. Don't take me anywhere out of the strip mall or anything. I might get jet lag.* "See you then."

IN CORAL GABLES, Barrington stared at his own phone, which was attached to the same line he'd just used to fax three possible code violations through to his attorney. He felt a little sick. Flowers?

I am such a bastard.

Had he really just asked her to go to dinner with him? And at Benito's? The words had popped out of his mouth without him really thinking about it. Benito knew he was the new landlord. Troy would just have to pray he wouldn't out him.

But that was really the least of his concerns. Was it fair of Troy to eat with her, joke with her, laugh with her, *sleep* with her—when the whole time he was essentially plotting against her?

When he found a way to break the lease, she was going to hate him. There was no doubt about that.

The problem was that he really wanted to see her again, no matter how he tried to talk himself out of it.

Troy told himself that none of his actions had been premeditated. That he hadn't meant to take things with Peggy so far. He wouldn't have let it happen with any other woman, but there was just something about her. She was half tough and half vulnerable. Half glamour and half pragmatism. And she'd fought her way onto a college football team, which impressed the hell out of him.

All of that and the gorgeous red hair, the unbelievably curvy body and the mind-blowing sex…. Could he really blame himself for weakening and asking her out again?

Troy told himself that really, the damage was done. After all, he couldn't unsleep with her now. So did sleeping with her again make things all that much worse?

He tried to snap his focus back to his own future and his agenda of owning a sporting goods store. He wasn't a rich, big cheese anymore. He had to make a living. *It's just business, nothing personal.*

But somehow he'd gone and made it *very* personal, hadn't he? And at some point, there'd be hell to pay.

He tried to refocus on the mounds of paper in front of him, but his concentration was shot. Not only was he a jerk, but…possessive instincts that he had no right to have about Peggy kicked in. Who the hell had sent her flowers? And was it reasonable for Troy to beat the shit out of him?

9

PEGGY NOW EYED the mysterious flower arrangement as if it were a grove of Venus flytraps. She really didn't care who it was from if it wasn't from Troy. In fact, it began to give her the creeps.

Who else would spend so much money, make an overblown statement like that? Did she have a real stalker?

At three-thirty, when she had to leave for her coaching gig, she wrestled the Amazonian flower arrangement off of the kitchen table and struggled down the hallway with it, narrowly escaping being poked in the eye by a particularly vicious bird of paradise "beak."

She emerged at the reception area and told Shirlie that she'd be back.

"What, you can't bear to be separated from your flowers? You're going to drive them to the middle school and then the take-out window at Taco Bell?"

"Turns out they're not from Troy. I don't know who they're from, and I don't like it. So I'm dropping them at the hospital."

Shirlie blanched in horror. "You can't just…get rid of those gorgeous flowers!"

"Yes, I can. Some sick person will enjoy them a lot more than I do."

Ignoring Shirlie's outrage, Peg hauled them outside and set them on the hood of her Mini Cooper while she hunted for her keys. She found them, unlocked the passenger-side door and wrestled the arrangement into the front seat of the tiny car, dislodging a foam rock and some moss in the process. Then, after a couple of delightful jabs in the ear with another bird's beak, she zoomed off.

A hospital volunteer gladly took the mini rain forest to cheer up patients in the oncology ward, and Peg tried to put her secret admirer out of her mind.

But even on the middle-school's practice field, she found herself eyeing a lanky maintenance man and a stoop-shouldered stay-at-home dad as the potential culprits.

Why, she asked herself as she put the girls through a series of sprints and agility exercises, *am I so cynical that I automatically assume the flowers are from a weirdo? Why can't I believe they're from a nice person who just wanted to brighten my day?*

Because there are too many not-so-nice people out there.

She looked out at the girls on the field, her heart softening at the gangly limbs, the braces, the beginnings of some adolescent acne. A few of them had training bras and wore cosmetics and even got periods, while others were freshly scrubbed, wide-eyed and still forbidden to get their ears pierced.

All of them would eventually develop into young women, encounter men and confusing relationships. She couldn't protect them, couldn't live their lives for them. But she could give them the gift of athletic competence and foster their self-esteem—so that they had the tools to do battle in what was still so often a man's world.

No one had prepared her for the nastiness and resentment that occurred when, for example, a woman dared to usurp a man's position on a college football team.

While most of her teammates had been outwardly polite, if not warmly welcoming, she'd sensed an underlying current of contempt. And that was before the really ugly incident…the one she couldn't ignore. The reason she'd walked away for good.

Peggy shoved the past out of her mind, blew her whistle and gathered the girls around her. "Okay, ladies, good job on the sprints! Let's work on some skills training for about ten minutes now, and then we'll scrimmage. Brianna, Cathy and Dara—I want you focused on blocking.

"Jody, Liz and Kimmie, pay attention to footwork and tip skills. Laura, you work on getting clear so that Danni can pass to you, and Danni, whatever you do, don't get sacked. How's that knee, Jen? You holding up okay? I don't want you to overextend it again."

She had no time to think about Troy, or their awkwardness on the phone, or his feeble invitation to dinner. But later, on the drive back to the salon and in the blessed coolness of the showers there, she did mull over things.

If she hadn't called him first, would Troy have called her at all?

Why buy the cow when you can have the milk for free? Her aunt Thelma's old-fashioned saying popped into her head. Ridiculous in this day and age...but Peggy couldn't help thinking about her sex-to-football analogy.

It's easier this way—you don't have to worry about the downs—you just score.

And Troy's answer:

It's like the other team handing you the ball and inviting you over the goal line. That sucks.

She'd definitely invited him over her goal line, and he'd scored multiple orgasms. So perhaps the thrill of the chase was gone. Perhaps he didn't respect her, now that it was morning.

But why did it always boil down to the woman losing the guy's respect? What about *her* respect for the man? Why were women seen as giving something up, rather than receiving something that they wanted? She liked the modern-day response to the free-milk adage: *Why buy the whole pig when all you want is a little sausage?*

Peggy decided she was a freewheeling woman in charge of her own sexuality and her own life...and her very atypical mother would be proud.

Speaking of her mother, she hadn't talked to her at all lately. She wondered what kind of crazy poem or performance art piece Mom was working on now.

She only spoke in rhyme and she only wore green, varying shades of green ranging from chartreuse to hunter. The last time Peg had seen her, she'd been in an olive phase. But who knew? She might have moved on to teal or emerald by now.

Mom had been divorced for years, ever since Peggy and Hal's father had shacked up with a dolphin trainer from Sea World. It was then that her mother had lapsed into rhyme as a way of expressing herself…. Peggy understood her, but everyone else just assumed she'd had a mental breakdown.

Of course, everyone who knew their family had always thought Peg's brother, Hal, teetered on a fine line between genius and madness, too. So she'd looked like the normal one, even if she'd pursued an all-male sport with an intensity their community didn't understand.

Peg pulled her cell phone out of her bag and dialed her mother's number, wanting advice, but her mom didn't answer. She didn't bother leaving a message.

Suddenly she decided that what she really needed was a male point of view. Where was Alejandro? She tracked him down in the small, windowless office that he used for doing paperwork.

"Alejandro?"

"Yes, *chica?*"

"Give me the male point of view on this situation. I spent last night with a guy—"

"You slut," he teased.

She ignored that. "The guy and I had a great time. This morning that arrangement of flowers came. But when I called to thank him, he said he didn't send them. Then, to make it worse, he asked me out, but almost as if he didn't want to, as if he was just being polite. What does it mean?"

Alejandro pursed his lips. "Is he married?"

Horrible thought. Had she spent all last night having wild monkey sex with somebody's husband? No. Somehow she just knew he wasn't married.

"I don't think there's a wife anywhere in the picture."

"Then maybe you just caught him at a bad time."

"No, I think it was more than that."

"Maybe you sprained his Mr. Happy and he's in pain."

"Alejandro, be serious!"

"Okay, okay. Maybe he's just shy."

Peggy reminisced about some of the things Troy had done to her last night. "He's definitely not shy."

"Well then, I'd say he was just a jerk who got some of your aunt Thelma's free milk and isn't thirsty anymore, but he did ask you out again. So, what's to worry about, except who did send the flowers?"

"Alejandro, listen to me. His tone of voice was weird. He was kind of cool toward me."

"Peggy, you women overanalyze these things to death. This could be as simple as he doesn't like taking personal calls at work. What does he do?"

It was a damn good question. Peggy couldn't believe she didn't know the answer to that. She'd have to ask him.

By the time she left Alejandro's office, she felt better. But she still didn't know who'd sent her the damn flowers.

"SO, WHAT DO YOU DO, Troy?" Peggy asked him as they sat at a table at Benito's. The place was dark and simply furnished with long wooden picnic tables and benches; squat green candles set at two-foot intervals along them. You didn't want to come to Benito's in a tight skirt, since sitting down required a bit of climbing. Luckily, Peg had worn a loose-fitting jean skirt today. It was short, but she could maneuver in it.

Benito's was slightly cheesy, but cheesy in a charming way. Plastic pizza-wedge lighting blinked on and off around a large open window to the kitchen, where Benny's high-school-age son would occasionally amuse kids and himself by juggling meatballs or twirling pizza dough. If his mother, Claudia, caught him with the meatballs, she'd whack him in the butt with whatever came to hand: a cooking spoon, a rolling pin, a box of spaghetti.

Peggy rested her elbows on the red-and-white-checkered tablecloth, looking up surreptitiously every once in a while. Benito and Claudia had hung Chianti bottles over all the tables, intertwined with fake grape vines. She couldn't get rid of the fear that one of the bottles would fall on her head and knock her unconscious. She might even pitch forward into the candle in the center of the table, catching her hair on fire.

Troy repeated her question. "What do I do?" He looked vaguely uncomfortable. "I, um…well, I'm retired from the Jaguars and I decided to quit coaching after I left Gainesville, which was only a month ago. So I'm kind of…taking a break to work on my house in the Gables. And I'm planning to open a sporting goods store."

The awkwardness that had pervaded their phone conversation was still present. Peggy took a sip of the Cabernet she'd ordered.

"A sporting goods store! How cool. So will it be here in Miami? Have you found a location yet?"

His own glass at his lips, Troy had started to nod at the first question and then began to cough.

"You okay? Need me to pound on your back?"

He nodded, then shook his head, continuing to hack and wheeze. Finally he gasped, "Wine down the wrong pipe."

She wrinkled her nose in sympathy. "Oooh, don't you hate that?"

He nodded, still recovering.

"So when are you going to open this sporting goods store?"

"Oh, you know. I'm hoping by next year. There's a lot of, uh, legwork to be done. And a lot of numbers to crunch."

"Will you specialize in anything?" Peggy asked. "You could sponsor some of the kids' teams around here—you know, donate the uniforms. It would be good PR for you, and I happen to know of a certain powder-puff team that could use some new stuff, especially helmets. I can't wait to ask you to price pink helmets by the dozen, Barrington." She grinned at him, but he didn't grin back.

Finally he did muster a smile. "Yeah. Well, we'll have to see how it goes. Of course, since I'm the coach of my nephew's team, they'll get first dibs." He winked.

Peggy put her hands on her hips. "Oh, really? But you have *two nieces* on *my* team. I'd think that their equipment would be equally important to you."

Troy raised his brows. "Pink helmets? Are those

really necessary? Besides, what's wrong with their existing ones? I can't supply the equipment for every youth team in Miami, and let's face it, the boys are a little more rough-and-tumble than the girls."

Peggy's temples started throbbing. "That is so untrue. My girls are every bit as aggressive—and talented, I might add—as your boys! I'd put the ladies on the field any day and they'd kick your butts."

"Is that so." His body language became cocky and competitive: shoulders back and chin up.

"Yeah, that *is* so." Her chin came up, too.

"Uh-huh." Troy smirked. "Well, I think your strength lies more in color coordination. That's why Danni and Laura and the rest of the puff team painted their nails before their last game—because matching team polish really brings out the beast in them."

Peggy narrowed her eyes on him. "That was a team spirit thing, and I can't believe you'd be so snarky about your own nieces. You obviously don't take them or their talent seriously."

"Yes, I do," Troy protested. "I didn't mean it that way. I just meant that the guys are rougher. They'll need the helmets more, especially as they get a little older and things get serious for them. Let's face it, most of the girls won't go on to play in high school."

Peggy gritted her teeth. "Because nobody takes them seriously and nobody *encourages* them to play in high school. They're pushed to try out for cheerleader instead."

Troy put his hands up, palm out. "Hey, don't get all mad at me. I know that you were different, okay, and I admire you for that. But the majority of girls have no interest in doing what you did."

Peg took a deep breath and counted to three. "Let's just change the subject. Because if we don't, I might be tempted to shove those bread sticks where the sun don't shine, buddy."

"God, I love it when women threaten me with violence. It makes me all horny," Troy teased her. "What bread sticks?"

She glared at him. "The ones Benito's bringing to us right now. Hi, Benny!" She turned to the restaurateur with a sunny smile. "How are you?"

"Very well, *grazie*. You?" Benito placed a large napkin-covered basket in the center of their table. The aroma of hot bread wafted out, hot bread liberally spread with garlic butter. Peggy's mouth watered, and Benito beamed at her. He gestured toward Troy.

"I see you have dinner with our so-handsome landlord! Should help with the rent, eh?" He winked and laughed. "*Ciao*, Mr. Barrington. You like-a more wine?"

"*Landlord?*" Peggy stared at Troy.

Troy shrugged and looked sheepish.

"He no tell you? He inherit whole strip mall from his uncle, Newton Baines. When, one month ago, you say?"

Troy nodded.

Peggy felt like an idiot. She'd called the cops on their landlord? "Why…"

"Benito, I'd sure love to take you up on that second glass of wine. How about one for the lady, too?"

"Right away, Signor B.!"

"I didn't tell you because I didn't want to make you uncomfortable," Troy said quickly, after Benito left. "About the whole stalking thing, or like you had to go out with me since I owned the place."

She shoved her embarrassment away. "I wouldn't have. I already told you, your money doesn't intimidate me."

His mouth twisted. "Trust me, there's not as much money anymore. Three college funds, my sister's retirement fund and a bunch of property, and it takes a mint to maintain that."

"Well," she said coolly, finishing her glass of Cabernet, "After Hours must be quite the cash cow for you." Oh, hell. How had she gotten back to cows and milk again?

Troy crunched down on a bread stick and didn't answer. She supposed her comment had been tacky. This evening was going all wrong, and she didn't know how to salvage it. Didn't know if she even wanted to, after his comments about girls and football.

She knew Troy spoke the truth about how many girls went on to play high school or college ball, but it irritated her that he saw no need to change the status quo. That he was fine with girls being cheerleaders, supporting their male football teams. It made her want to scream.

"Tell you what, Mr. Landlord," she said. "We're gonna challenge you guys to a game toward the end of the season. And you are going to eat your words. Then you're gonna owe us the helmets *and* new uniforms. Not to mention pink cleats for the whole team."

"Deal," he said. "But can I ask you something? If

you're so eager for your *ladies* to be taken seriously, why not lighten up on the pink?"

"Because I'm making a point. You're about to suggest that they shave their heads, maybe get nose rings and tattoos just to look tough, aren't you?"

"No."

She ignored him. "Well, they're not going to do that. My girls are going to look as feminine as they please while kicking ass. They're going to pulverize the opposition after touching up their lipstick! I'm so *sick* of these stereotypes—that if women are good at sports, they've gotta look butch. Not true."

"Okay, calm down," Troy said, pulling the napkin-covered basket toward him. "I'd offer you a bread stick, but I'm afraid of what you might do with it."

That got a smile out of her, but she nodded. "Damn straight."

"You're a tough one, Peggy-Sue. I have a feeling that any moment now you'll challenge me to swords, pistols or bread sticks at dawn." He grinned that irresistible grin of his, the one where both dimples flashed.

"On guard," she said. "Watch out for the garlic."

Benito appeared with their second glasses of wine and took their orders, chicken cacciatore for her and manicotti for Troy. They both chose the Caesar salad.

"A good thing if there's any kissing later," Troy pointed out. "We'll *both* have the breath of camels."

"Kissing?" She raised her glass to her lips and flooded her mouth with the tart Cabernet. "Aren't you presuming a lot?"

He avoided her gaze. "Yeah, I guess I am. And I shouldn't."

She set her glass down. "Why did you ask me to dinner, Troy? Because I could swear that you had no intention of doing it. All that stuff about how you wanted to get to know me, and then when I called, you didn't seem pleased to hear from me."

He swore under his breath and ran a hand through his close-cropped hair. "Peggy, it's not that. Believe it or not, I was thrilled when you called."

"Yeah, you were turning cartwheels. Come on, Troy!" Encouraged by the wine, she leaned forward and said in low tones, "Just go ahead and give me the speech about how it's not me, it's you, or tell the truth and say that since we had our sex-a-thon, you don't respect me anymore. Because I must be loose, and while you might screw that kind of woman, you sure don't want to date her—"

"Peggy—"

"You already got a bucket of free milk, so why tow around the cow—"

"Hey! That is complete bullshit—"

"Right, of course it is. Then give me your version."

"Damn, woman! Look, I like you a lot. You're smart, you're beautiful, you're challenging and you turn me on like you wouldn't believe. But the thing is that you're also my nieces' coach. And when you called I was just thinking that it's not a good idea to take this any further. That's all."

"Then why did you ask me to dinner?"

"Because I wanted to anyway, even though it's probably not smart. You're an amazing woman, Peggy. I like to look at you, I like to talk with you, and I damn sure like to touch you...."

Heat blossomed all over her skin, and she felt foolish. She'd just behaved like a raving lunatic, but Troy still sat opposite her instead of storming out. He had a perfectly reasonable explanation for his hesitance on the phone.

A waiter, not Benito this time, appeared at the table. "Cacciatore?"

She nodded, and he placed the dish before her.

"And manicotti for *signor.*"

Troy thanked him.

Dinner was served, and Peggy was intensely grateful to be able to concentrate on her food. What were she and Troy going to talk about next? They'd already covered sex. Might as well move on to the other taboo subjects: politics and religion.

Then he turned the tables on her. "So, Peggy-Sue. If you didn't think I really wanted to ask you out to dinner, then why did you accept my invitation?"

10

TROY ASKED THE QUESTION partly to make her squirm after her tirade, and partly because he really wanted to know the answer.

Peggy avoided his gaze, finished chewing her bite of chicken cacciatore and pushed a piece of zucchini around her plate before she answered. "Because I wanted to see you again."

He smiled. "And why would you want to see me?"

"Well, you're not the ugliest guy I've ever taken back to my apartment."

"Thank you," he said, hugely entertained. "And?"

"You left your lips at my place and I wanted to return them to you."

"That's so generous. A man with no lips is a tragic sight. He'd never be able to kiss another woman."

"Yeah, and I was worried about that."

"So when are you going to give my lips back? Where are they, in your tote bag?"

"Nope."

"Tucked in your bra?"

"Nope, not there, either."

His smile widened. "Oh, lower down, then?"

Her white teeth flashed. "Yup. They're all puckered up and I'm sitting on them."

Troy choked. "Are you trying to tell me that I'm kissing your freckled little ass?"

"It's the natural order of things, dude."

"I am *so* going to enjoy punishing you for this later."

She laughed. "Promises, promises. Maybe you'll get the chance, and maybe not. My aunt Thelma would say you got way too much free milk last night."

"Correct me if I'm wrong, but I figure you'd get upset if I tried to pay you for it."

Peggy threw her napkin at him.

"So that's not what Aunt Thelma is suggesting?"

"Not exactly."

Benito came over to ask if their food was okay, and they assured him that it was delicious. He brought them each another glass of wine without asking.

"You trying to get us drunk, Benny?" Peggy asked.

"*Sì,* so you can take advantage of him."

Troy could think of nothing he'd like better. His appetite right now was not for food, it was for Peggy. Forget scruples and ethics and all that...he wanted to reach across the table and pull her into his arms. He wanted her ripe, soft mouth; he wanted her full breasts filling his hands, her pink nipples thrusting against his palms.

He wanted her lips on his cock and her sweet ass riding him, urgency filling her as much as he did. He wanted to be sliding into her hot, wet body, smell her desire and hear her gasps and whimpers in his ear as he sent her into a frenzy.

Jesus. He had to get a hold of himself—they were sitting in a public restaurant, and he was so hard he could knock a plank off the table.

Opposite him, Peggy picked up a bread stick and met his eyes as she brought it to her mouth. Christ, she was reading him like a book. Her eyes slanted like a cat's, she darted out the tip of her tongue and licked at the end of the bread. She wrapped her lips around it and pulled gently. Then she slid it halfway into her mouth, caressing the bottom of the stick with her tongue.

"I'm so gonna make you pay for this," Troy said hoarsely.

Peggy bit the end off the bread stick. "Mmm."

That was when he felt something sliding against his crotch. Troy grabbed it and found that it was her small renegade foot.

Her eyes on his, her hand still wrapped around the bread stick, she flashed him a wicked smile. "Sporting wood, are we? Naughty, naughty." She nudged his balls with her toe, and that was the last straw.

Troy gripped her ankle, forced her foot up and searched for some kind of revenge that was acceptable in the middle of a restaurant. He began to tickle the bottom of Peggy's foot.

She had just the reaction he was looking for. She pulled hard to get away from him, banging her knee on the underside of the table and making the candles jump.

Troy smiled blandly and kept tickling.

She squeaked and yanked again, unable to get away. "Let go!" she snapped, dropping the bread stick.

"Why, little Miss Perv, are you ticklish? What a shame for you…should have thought of that before you started this, huh?"

"I hate you!"

"I know. It bothers me a lot, as you can see." He trailed his index finger from big toe to arch and then down to her heel, and she went nuts.

Peggy thrashed and gave a final mighty yank, just as he let go. She tumbled backward off the bench and onto the ceramic-tiled floor, still wearing only one shoe. He could see her blue satin underwear under the short jean skirt.

The other guests eyed her curiously, while Troy laughed so hard he almost blew the manicotti off his plate. "You okay?"

Peggy sat up just as Benito rushed over. "I'm fine, Benny. Thanks." She pushed the hair out of her face and sent Troy a Death Stare. "Our landlord just seems to have this effect on women."

THEY LEFT BY THE BACK DOOR, and as soon as it had shut Troy pinned her against the stucco wall of the building and took her mouth. The little witch was making him crazy. He would have swallowed her whole if he could have.

His hands roamed her breasts freely, moving up to cup them under her stretchy top. She moaned. Damn if he didn't want to take her right against the wall, here.

He slipped his fingers under her skirt and cupped her soft bottom, then dove lower and pulled aside the panties.

He fumbled at his fly, almost crazy with the desire to push inside her. He freed himself and pulled up her skirt.

She broke the kiss and pushed at his chest. "Someone might see us!"

"I find it so hard to care about that right now. And there's nothing back here but a five-foot fence and some sky." He stroked the soft wet folds between her legs and watched as her head fell back, felt her thighs begin to tremble. She was beautiful. And he wanted her right now.

She whimpered and her breathing turned shallow, came fast. Troy lifted her and sighed with satisfaction as her legs went automatically around his waist. He positioned her so that he probed her slick entrance and then thrust up in a single, almost savage motion.

She made a soft sound of shock and pleasure, and he slid his hands down to her bottom to support her, doing his best not to bang her against the wall as he stroked in and out of her. He felt like a caveman, was acting like one, too, and didn't care. She didn't appear to mind, and that was all that mattered. But…he really, really didn't want to stop and fish out a condom. "Birth control?" he gasped.

"Pill," she managed.

Relief filled him. "Let me see your breasts," he said, sliding in to the hilt again and knocking the breath out of her. Her hair was tumbled over her shoulders, hanging in her eyes, which were half-closed with desire. She nodded, her lower lip caught between her teeth.

He bent forward and took it between his own, wanting to possess everything about her. He wanted her body and soul, completely at his mercy. "Let me see," he said again once he'd released her mouth.

She pushed up her top, pulled down her bra so that her breasts poked impudently over it. Troy pulled out just enough so that he could bend his head to them, capture a nipple between his lips and suck hard. She cried out, he released it and drove into her. He worked her into a frenzy; she met his thrusts with the same urgency; until he hit some nerve deep inside of her. She gasped, arched her back and convulsed against him, shaking.

Just the sight of her, the feel of her losing control sent him over the edge, too. He pushed himself as far as he could into her sweetness and heat and spilled himself inside her, cursing softly.

He stood like that, embedded in her, until he realized how uncomfortable she must be, and gently lifted her off him, setting her on her feet. She automatically straightened her clothes, probably still fearing discovery, but not even a mosquito seemed to have witnessed their public indecency.

He noticed that her thighs were shaking and she could barely stand up. He gathered her in his arms, pulling her against him. He kissed her hair. "You okay? I'm sorry I was rough—I don't know what got into me."

"I wanted it rough," she said into his chest. She bit his nipple through his shirt, bit it hard.

"Ow!"

Peggy tipped back her head and smiled at him in the darkness. "Where are we going for round two, cowboy?"

SHE RODE HIM in the moonlight on his freshly screened back porch. His entire yard was surrounded by a virtually impenetrable ficus hedge, ten feet high. It was one of the few things he liked about the place, since it offered total privacy.

The scents of sex, new wood and citrusy lantana mingled with the night air. A touch of chlorine from the pool intruded, too.

But mostly what he smelled was her: a green-apple eau de parfum, a honey-coconut shampoo, a tinge of sporty deodorant and the rich, natural musk of her body's secret places.

He lifted her easily, in spite of her protests, and rolled her under him, pinning her with his big body. Then he ate every succulent inch of her, drawing her flesh into his mouth and savoring it.

Feeding at the juncture of her thighs, he reduced her to begging before he rolled her onto her stomach and settled his cock in the cleft of her buttocks. He slipped his fingers down, found her lips and parted them. Then he thrust into her once again, unbelievably turned on when she raised her bottom to meet him, taking her weight on her knees.

She raised her torso on her hands, too, and her heavy, lush breasts swung free. He reached around her waist for them and pleasured them as he stroked into her, pulled out, rammed himself in again until he thought he'd die from the sheer ecstasy of it.

He squeezed her breasts gently, toyed with the nipples until she arched her back, cried out and ground against the root of him, body trembling and convulsing around him. He thrust two, three more times—and then collapsed over her, murmuring her name.

THEY WENT SKINNY-DIPPING afterward, bodies slipping through the cool, silky water. It soothed all the parts of them that were oversensitized, allayed some of the burning that Peggy felt between her legs. Troy's body looked even bigger submerged in the water, her own small and white beside him.

There was a shelf at the deep end of the pool, and he tugged her over to it, then into his lap. He folded his arms around her and they sat in the water listening to the night noises: the wind in the trees, the cicadas in song, the frogs' amphibian baritone.

This is as close as it gets to heaven on earth.

She snuggled back against his hard chest, feeling safe and protected and thoroughly sexed-out. She didn't think about the future much, just that Troy had been sweet to have concerns about dating his nieces' coach. That showed a rare, old-fashioned honor that you didn't see much these days....

She gazed inside at his house, which he laughingly referred to as the hovel. It wasn't one, but the ancient old-person furnishings like the avocado-green couch and the gold-and-orange-and-brown crocheted afghan hadn't been what she'd expected.

She'd thought his living room would be dominated by

a massive wide-screen television, wall-to-wall carpet and a big, ugly black leather couch. Nothing could be further from the truth. The floors were scarred pine and the TV was a relic from the 1960s, tiny and sporting rabbit-ear antennae that made it look like a martian's suitcase.

The kitchen was something out of a time warp, too: old-fashioned cabinets with 1950s handles, an unspeakable stove and a refrigerator that she'd swear was powered by squirrels running on a wheel. The only "modern" addition was a gray plastic answering machine, its wires trailing from the wall-mounted phone.

The slick decorator-chosen furnishings of most pro ball players weren't in evidence. No bearskin or tigerhead rug. No trophy case. No revolving round bed under a mirror.

"Where are your things?" she asked him. "These must have come with the house."

"Gorgeous, aren't they?" He chuckled. "All my stuff's in storage. I'll bring it in when I'm done remodeling the place. We'll be making a huge mess, knocking out walls and redoing the roofline. I'd rather trash the poor old geezer's furniture than mine—and I have to sit on something."

"So we're both making a new start," Peggy said. "You came down here from Gainesville, I came down here from Connecticut."

"Yeah," he said. "I never want to be financially dependent on the whims of a team owner or an athletic program again."

She had to ask. "So did you leave a girlfriend behind?"

His arms stiffened. "No. No girlfriend. There were a few women who kept trying out for the position, though."

She slid under his arms and under the water. When she surfaced, she shook water out of her eyes. Treading water, she said, "Trying out for the position?"

He shrugged. "I know how arrogant that sounds. Sorry. But it's true. There hasn't been a shortage of women in my life, most of them annoying and with no identities of their own. They want me to validate them somehow, and that disgusts me. I don't want to be used—not for money, not for status, not for an identity. I guess that's the reason I'm still single and most of my old teammates are married." Troy changed the subject, unwilling to dwell on the fact that he no longer had money or status. Now he was just a guy who mowed his own lawn, like everyone else.

"So why did you come down here from Yankeeland?"

She rolled onto her back in the water and stared up at the stars. "To get away from the stupid, lying bastard whom I almost married."

"Care to share any details?"

"B-league hockey player, steroid user, gambler, loser. Replaced the stone in my engagement ring with a "nicer" one, a big honking CZ. But I knew about his gambling debts and figured it out."

"Nice."

"Yeah. The funny thing is, I never even wanted a diamond in the first place. I'm not really into that stuff. But Eddie insisted. I think he didn't want to look bad in front of his friends. Of course, he ended up looking worse than he could have imagined—though a couple of them called me a bitch and couldn't understand why, if I never wanted a rock in the first place, I'd be bothered by a fake one. Eddie drove around with a bumper sticker on his Saab after that—'Why buy her a diamond? She won't live forever.'"

"God. The guy sounds like a real charmer."

"Irresistible. I pine after him to this day," Peg said dryly. She rolled to her stomach again and dove under the water. When she surfaced again, she told Troy, "It ended up being the best thing that ever happened to me. I love it here, the kooky mix of people, the internationalism, the sun and water. You've got the beach bums in their flip-flops, the show-offs dripping diamonds and designer duds, the students with their backpacks, the moms with their toddlers and the old guys with their cigars and Guayabera shirts." She swam down the length of the pool, doing an easy sidestroke.

On the return lap, she continued. "What I love most, though, is being part of After Hours. We have a little community there, whacky as it may be. It's our corner of the world where we get to have fun working and make other people feel good. Transform them sometimes, other times just maintain their sanity in a crazy existence…a manicure can lift a woman's spirits for the rest of her day. Or a great haircut. We get models coming in here on their way to the clubs, but we also get exhausted moms who wouldn't make it through their weeks without a massage. I have one who can only afford it every six weeks or so, on the change she collects in a jar. She can't tip much, but I adore her. It makes *me* feel good to make *her* feel good."

Troy had an odd expression on his face and his gaze had grown distant. "Peggy," he said, "I need to tell you—" He broke off as the phone rang inside the screen porch. "Who the hell is calling me at 1:00 a.m.? This can't be good."

He hoisted himself over the edge of the pool and strode, wet and naked, toward the porch. She was riveted by his body, sleek and silvery in the moonlight. The broad shoulders, the long lean legs, the powerful musculature of the whole. *Maybe I hate jocks and football players, but I sure do like to look at them nude.*

"Hello?" Troy answered the phone. "Samantha, what's wrong?" He swore. "Call the cops!" He listened a moment more. "You know what? There comes a time when you just can't worry about that. He's doing it to himself. Call them." He swore again. "I'll be right there."

"Troy?"

"I have to go. My asshole brother-in-law has just shown up at my sister's house drunk. He's trying to kick in the door, and she won't call the cops because of the kids. Anyway, it's still half his property, so I don't know what the cops could do unless he's actually threatening her or them. Right now all he's trying to do is *see* them."

"I'll come with you." She was out of the pool already, and hunting for her clothes on the porch.

"You don't want to get involved in this."

"The girls—maybe I can help with them."

"Sam's there, and she's their mother." He was already headed for the door, keys in hand.

Peggy ran after him, half-dressed. "She may not be able to handle her own emotions, much less theirs!"

"Fine. Whatever." Even under these circumstances, he opened the passenger-side door for her, though he almost threw her inside. They were squealing out of his driveway in seconds.

She finished dressing in the car, and pulled her hair back into a ponytail with a rubber band she found in her tote. Troy's face had set into hard lines, his jaw clenched.

"Does your brother-in-law have a gun?"

He shook his head. "I don't think so. Christ, I hope not."

"Has he ever raised a hand to your sister?"

"His specialty has always been punching holes through drywall and occasionally turning furniture into projectiles. He's never actually hit her or the kids. But he's drunk, and he's stupid, and I don't like this situation at all. He disappeared on them seven months ago, and I wish like hell he'd stayed gone."

Peggy echoed his sentiment. As she clung to the seat while they careened around corners and broke the speed limit, all she could think about was Danni and Laura and their brother, the helpless child victims in this situation.

She felt a soul-deep rage at men who terrorized and hurt the women and children in their lives, and quite frankly she hoped that Troy, who appeared to be one of the good guys, would beat the living snot out of his brother-in-law. Maybe it wouldn't solve anything, but it would sure be satisfying.

11

"STAY HERE," Troy ordered Peggy. He erupted out of the car and shot over the sidewalk, up the steps and into the house he'd parked in front of. It was a neat little bungalow on a postage-stamp lawn, painted a soft blue with white trim. A familiar Nissan Pathfinder sat in the driveway, the car that Samantha used to pick up the twins from powder-puff practice. Blocking it in was a shiny black Dodge Ram truck with inordinately big tires; Peg surmised that it belonged to Sam's husband.

Peggy got out of the car despite Troy's instructions and stood in front of the place, her heart feeling as if it were hurling itself against the wall of her chest. Were Danni and Laura okay? Was their brother okay? Was Sam okay? How violent had this altercation gotten while she and Troy were driving over?

A lower left panel of the door was splintered, leaving a gaping hole, but there was no damage around the lock or the jamb.

It looked to Peggy as if Sam had let her husband—ex-husband?—inside, maybe to get him calmed down, or maybe so that the neighbors wouldn't call the police.

From inside the house she heard shouting. She moved to a window and tried to peer in through the half-closed blinds, making out Troy's big body near an overturned armchair. He had another shaggy-haired man in a lock, his forearm across the guy's throat. "Get the hell out of here and don't come back, or I will pulverize you and then snap your neck like a chicken bone."

"Troy, don't hurt him!" Samantha, blond hair wild and cheeks tearstained, cowered in a far corner of the room, wearing nothing but boxer shorts and a T-shirt.

The smaller man called her something vile and told Troy to do something anatomically impossible. Peggy winced and hoped the kids weren't hearing this, but she knew they must be. Where were they? Hiding under their beds, poor things?

"You can't keep me off my own property, you son of a bitch!" The shaggy man snarled, trying to twist free. "And you can't stop me from seeing my kids."

Troy's answer was to haul the man by the neck to the door. "You can see your kids during reasonable hours, when you're sober. In the meantime, you piece of shit, get away from them and get away from my sister."

The guy scrabbled ineffectively against Troy's grip, kicked backward and even tried to turn and bite him. "I'll file assault charges, damn you!"

"You do what you have to do. The cops can come out here and take a look at the door you were kicking in. They can ask Sam and your kids a few questions. And they can inspect you for nonexistent bruises. Believe me, I'd like to take your ass apart, but it's not going to do my sister any good to have me in jail."

Troy wrestled him off the porch and into the yard. Then he released his neck and gave him a kick in the pants that sent him sprawling. "Walk back to whatever roach motel you crawled out of."

"Give me my keys, you prick!"

"Oh, sure. Frankly, I'd love to see you wrap your car around a telephone pole, but in the state you're in, you'd take some innocent person with you. You're not getting behind the wheel, you're walking. And you start *now*." Troy took a menacing step toward him, and the guy stumbled to his feet. Still cursing, he lurched down the street.

Peggy expelled a breath she hadn't been aware she was holding. "Your sister has got to file a restraining order first thing in the morning."

"Yeah. You okay?"

She nodded. "I don't know if she is, though." She gestured toward the house. "And there's no way the children could have slept through this."

Samantha was huddled in a corner, crying. Troy ran to her, knelt and put his hands on her shoulders. "Sam, it's okay. Sam, where are the kids?"

She raised a red, blotchy face. "Bathroom. I told them to lock themselves in the bathroom." She wiped her nose on the back of her hand and let Troy help her up. "Coach—Peggy—what are you doing here?"

Sam headed for the hallway and the bathroom, her

children her first priority, but embarrassment crept into her demeanor.

"Peggy and I were, uh, having coffee when you called."

Sam nodded, then knocked on the bathroom door. "Derek? Danni? Laura? It's okay now. He's gone. Uncle Troy is here."

It was Danni who opened it, her face pale. They'd all been crying. Sam and Troy hugged and kissed each one of them, and Peggy tried to swallow the lump in her throat.

Later, she made them hot chocolate in the kitchen while Troy persuaded Sam to give a statement to the police.

"It's really hard when parents don't get along and they split up," Peggy told the kids. "Mine did the same thing."

"Did your dad go away for almost a year and then show up yelling and kick in your door?" Laura asked.

Peggy put her arm around Laura and pulled her close. "No. My dad just got married to somebody else. But it sucked, because he also got a whole new family, and we were afraid he liked that one better."

"Did he?" It was Derek who asked this question.

I have to be careful how I answer this. "Um, no. Not better. But my dad was a very athletic guy, kind of like your uncle Troy. And this new family of his had a boy who was also very athletic. My brother, Hal, was a competitive swimmer, but my dad liked football. So he went to Alan's games a lot."

"Alan was the new boy?" Danni asked.

"Yes."

"What about your games? Did he go to those?"

Peggy ruffled Derek's hair. "Not so much. I was a girl, and he didn't think my games were that important."

"That's really unfair. He hurt your feelings."

Peggy nodded. "He did. But I don't think he meant to. Just like I don't think *your* dad meant to scare you tonight. He just drank too much whiskey or something and felt guilty for going away. So, not thinking straight, he decided he wanted to see you at one o'clock in the morning. And of course that's way past your bedtime."

"I hate him," said Derek, pushing his hot chocolate away. "He said really bad things to my mom when she wouldn't open the door."

"Sometimes people say things they don't mean." Peggy prayed she was handling this right.

"I think he meant them. Even without whiskey he used to be a jerk." Derek's eyes were hard and angry. "I was glad when he went off."

Laura and Danni didn't say anything. But the guilt on their faces spoke for them. Peggy wished she could say something, anything, to comfort these children. "It's okay to be mad at your dad," she began. "It doesn't mean that you don't still love him."

"I don't want to love him," Danni blurted.

Peggy stroked her hair. "Yeah, but you probably do."

"He doesn't deserve it."

Peggy sighed and stroked the girl's cheek. "Well, that's the funny thing about love. You can't help how you feel about people, whether they deserve it or not."

TROY EVENTUALLY CALLED a cab for Peggy, since he didn't feel he could leave Sam and the kids alone. Mr. Creep might return. "I'm sorry the evening ended like this," he said. "And I'm sorry I can't take you back to your car personally. You make the driver wait until you're inside with the doors locked, okay?"

"I'll be fine."

"I mean it."

"Thanks for dinner, even if I embarrassed you by falling off the bench."

He gave her a tired grin. "Hey, I could care less. It's not me who showed my blue panties to Benito."

She winced.

"I had a great time earlier tonight. I want to see you again…. There's something we should talk about, though." He passed a hand over his eyes, rubbing at them with the heel of it.

"Troy. You deal with your family situation and don't worry about anything else for the time being. You know where to find me once things are more settled. After Hours isn't going anywhere."

He didn't say anything for a long moment. "Yeah."

The cab pulled up and Troy handed her into the back-seat, passing some cash to the driver once she was settled. "Troy, I can pay my own cab fare…."

He ignored her, gave the cabbie the address and then dropped a quick kiss on her mouth. "See you soon, Peggy-Sue. Don't run off and get married."

She rolled her eyes. "Fat chance of that. I've seen all I want of domestic bliss tonight."

PEGGY DIDN'T EVEN TRY to go into her bedroom when she got home, since she knew she couldn't sleep. Her apartment seemed particularly sterile, after the ugly but somewhat endearing geezer furnishings of Troy's place. Peggy sat cross-legged on the pristine taupe carpet and stared at Marly's painting on her wall. The girl on the faux television screen stared back at her, midkick. Her red hair flew in the breeze, her jersey slid askew against her body and her athletic pants were dirtied with smudges. The ultimate tomboy, she didn't look like the kind of girl who'd ever work in a salon and day spa.

Peg twisted her mouth wryly, dug her bare toes into the carpet and started going through the mail she'd grabbed on her way in.

She discarded a flyer encouraging her to buy a house from a man with a smarmy smile, a notification for the previous resident that her cat was due for shots and a department store catalogue filled with all sorts of things she didn't need and couldn't afford.

She did open a couple of bills and a letter from the school where she coached. She scanned it, her disbelief turning to anger.

Dear Ms. Underwood,
We regret to inform you that the school's athletic field will be undergoing improvements in the next few months, since we can expect relatively dry weather at this time of the year and must finish the process before the rainy season.

The school board has made the decision to move all of Woodward's athletic activities—practice and games—to the fields at the Coral Gables Youth Center. Since there are hundreds of teams utilizing these facilities, we have been given specific time slots in which to hold our activities, and there are not enough to go around.

For this reason, we must regretfully inform you that the girls' football program has been eliminated for the season. We realize that this may cause disappointment to both you and the young ladies affected by the decision. We look forward to the program resuming at some point next year, when the work on the athletic fields has been completed....

"What?" Peggy shouted aloud to the absent principal. "I don't see anything about the *boys'* program being eliminated!" It was the perfect ending to an already miserable evening: her pet project, meant to empower girls and teach them that there were no limits to what they could do, was being flushed.

12

TROY MADE SURE that Samantha's attorney filed a restraining order in the morning. He tried to get her to take the day off, but she insisted on going to work while he dropped the kids off at school.

Then he coolly took Mr. Creep's Dodge Ram to Home Depot and purchased another door, since the Lotus wasn't much use for hauling supplies. He figured the jerk was still sleeping off his hangover somewhere, and would never know. When he got back, he left a window down and the keys in the ignition. It wasn't his problem if the truck got stolen, and he didn't want his brother-in-law breaking into the house to find them.

He had popped the original door off its hinges and was hauling it around the side of the house when a bright blue Mini Cooper zoomed up, red hair flying out the driver's-side window. Peggy popped out of the munchkin-mobile like a cork from a champagne bottle—but her mood was anything but celebratory.

"Bastards!" she spat. "Chauvinist pigs from hell! Stupid assholes!" She waved a crumpled piece of paper at him, and then her eyes fell on the new door.

"Did Derek and the twins get any sleep? Sam? They doing better? The jerk didn't try to come back, did he?"

Troy absorbed the change of focus and emotion with calm amusement. "Derek slept. So did Sam. Danni and Laura not so well. But I'll make them take naps this afternoon and go to bed early. No, the jerk did not come back. Did you sleep? Judging from the purple bags under your eyes and the yawn that's pulling your mouth over your head at this moment, I'd say no. Now, what has you in such a lather?"

"I didn't sleep because I got this!" She waved the paper again, and he took it from her hand while she continued to rant. "You haven't received the notice from the school? That they're moving all the athletic teams to the youth center for practice and games?"

"I never opened my mail yesterday. Why are they doing this?" Troy started to read.

"They have canceled the girls' football league for the season! Because there aren't enough time slots at the center to go around! But do they eliminate the boys' program? Oh, no. Just the girls'!" Peggy was beside herself, practically hyperventilating. "It's just powder-puff, so it has no significance. It's expendable!"

Oh, boy. He finished scanning the letter and gave it back to her, frowning.

"They can't do this!" she said.

"Unfortunately, they can. A private school gets no state or federal funding, so they're not subject to the same rules that public schools are. What other teams got cut? Girls' softball? Any boys' activities?"

"I don't know—I haven't had a chance to look into it yet."

"Well, do me a favor. Help me get this door lined up so I can drop the pins into the hinges and then lock it. Then we'll go back to my place and make some calls."

"What about the back door?" she asked. "Does the creep have a key to that?"

"He doesn't have a key to anything anymore. Sam had the locks changed. I'll drop off a set of these to her on the way over to Coral Gables."

Peggy helped him line up the hinges on the new door, and dropped in the bottom pins while he got the top one in. Troy had to plane the wood slightly so that it would open and close easily.

She watched him as he worked, muscles in his arms flexing and sweat trickling down his back, disappearing into the waistband of his low-slung jeans. She traded in some of her anger for pure female appreciation and lust.

Troy's hair was still mussed from the previous night and he hadn't shaved: sawdust particles clung to some of his beard bristle, and even in his eyelashes. She resisted the urge to wipe his face for him—he probably wouldn't appreciate it.

He finished planing the door, opened and closed it with satisfaction, and then grabbed a broom to clean up the mess. She took it from him. "Let me do that, and you can put away your tools."

He raised a brow. "You're going to clean up after me? Hey, wanna do my laundry and make me some brownies, too?"

Peggy whacked him in the butt with the broom. He turned, grabbed it and used it to pull her toward him. "I was only kidding," he said against her mouth. Then he kissed her, sending sexual electricity shooting through her veins. She lost herself in his kiss for a while, as he stroked her tongue with his and explored every crevice of her mouth. She almost forgot her anger.

He smelled a little ripe, but she didn't care. His scent was all he-man, macho and competent. She didn't know why it turned her on that he could fix doors and replace porch floors, but it did.

Not that she had to get all girly about it. She was sure that she could nail planks to a deck and pop a precut door into a frame, too. So there. She broke the kiss, irritated with herself. *I can do anything he can.*

An irrelevant thought popped into her head. "Do you leave a toothbrush here at Sam's?" He'd tasted of mint.

"Not exactly." A smile crept onto his face. "I used Derek's after he left for school."

"Ugh!"

Troy shrugged. "It was better than dragon breath, and I figure what he doesn't know won't hurt him. You're not going to give me away, are you?"

"Depends."

He still had his hands on her shoulders, and they tightened in mock menace as he squinted down at her. "Depends on what?"

She thought about it for a second and then grinned impishly. "On your performance back at your place."

"My *performance?*"

She twisted away and ran laughing for her car, slamming the door and locking it just before he got to the driver's side.

He leered at her through the glass, his hands on his hips. "If you're brave enough to show up at my house after that little challenge, I'm gonna teach you something about performance."

"Ooooh, I hope so." Peggy turned the keys in the ignition and sped away. In her rearview mirror, she saw him sprint up the steps to lock Sam's door and then sprint back to the curb to get into the Lotus.

SHE WAS NAKED in his pool when he arrived and began to strip off his clothes purposefully. "You better watch out, little girl," he said. "Shark's almost in the water."

She turned to climb out as he dove in, but he was too fast. He caught her neatly by the ankle and jerked her backward. She shrieked and landed with an almighty splash, feeling his arm snake around her and then his hand between her legs. She surfaced sputtering, pushed the hair out of her eyes and said, "You don't wait for an invitation, do—oooh—you?"

"Oh, I think you issued that before you took off in that little munchkin-mobile of yours, honey. Excuse me, what was that?"

"*Aaaaaahhh.* Ohh, yes!"

"You're so agreeable all of a sudden."

"Not a munchkin—haahhhh—mobile!"

"It's no bigger than a doughnut," said Troy, flipping her onto her back and capturing a nipple in his mouth.

He squeezed her breasts together and licked back and forth at the tips, while she almost came on the spot. She tried to wrap her legs around him, but he wouldn't let her.

He raised his head and pushed her through the water over to the dual metal handrails on one side of the pool. "I think you'd better hang on to those, babe."

A little alarmed at his expression, she did. He pulled her body straight, so that she was floating on her back in the water. Then he parted her legs and walked between them. He cupped the cheeks of her bottom in his hands, squeezing gently and looking right at the core of her, which she found embarrassing in the bright sunlight. She wriggled and tried to move back so she could pull her knees together.

The cool water slapped at her sex, which felt divine. Everything was freer, more sensual in the water, cleaner.

Troy wouldn't let her budge more than six inches. "Where're you trying to go?" He growled. "I see something I want to eat."

A flash of heat streaked through her, causing the little bud at her center to throb almost painfully. The thought of his mouth on her, tongue flicking skillfully, suction applied just right...

He grinned at her wolfishly. "You want me to kiss you there, don't you?"

She swallowed and didn't reply, just closed her eyes halfway and willed him to do it.

"You want me to treat you like an ice-cream cone. Lick all around the edges, catch any drips, maybe take a little bite off the top now and then."

She was going to come from him just talking to her.

He dipped her down into the water and it lapped against her, coolness sliding and swirling along her hot flesh. She gasped and opened her thighs even wider, helpless under the promise of more pleasure.

Troy sank into the water so that the backs of her knees rested on his shoulders. She almost dug her heels into his back to urge him forward, but she was too inhibited. He wasn't her sex slave, after all! But heaven help her, she wanted him to be.

His hands moved all over her ass in the water, stroking and squeezing, fingers dipping into the cleft of her bottom and then moving along her inner thighs. She jerked to the side once or twice so that he'd touch her where she wanted to be touched, but he just laughed and moved quickly out of the way.

"You're torturing me," she said, her voice sounding plaintive to her own ears.

"You catch on fast."

"Please, Troy…"

"Please what?"

"Touch me."

"I am touching you."

She lost all shame and did dig her heels into his back. His only response was to chuckle softly. He lifted her bottom to the surface of the water and moved a little closer to her. Close enough to blow warm air there, while she arched her back mindlessly and tried to reach him.

He let her twist in the wind.

"Please," she moaned again.

"Please what? Say it. Say, 'Troy, I want you—'"

"Troy, I want you," she repeated hoarsely.

"To eat me."

She balked at that. "I can't say that, it's too dirty!"

"You can't say it, but you want me to do it."

"Yes," she whispered.

"Like this?" He licked her from the bottom of her sex to the top.

She gave a strangled cry.

He stabbed his tongue inside her, making circular motions, and she whimpered with mindless gratitude. Then he fastened his lips over her clitoris and sucked.

She came absolutely unglued, thrashing and crying out as wave after wave of sharp, tingling pleasure hit and crested over her.

He entered her on the last crescendo, in one stroke, and impossibly she came again, this time from somewhere deep inside, spasm after spasm while he drove into her, until she felt like a rag doll…and then felt nothing at all except for the blunt tip of him sliding in and out of her, the fullness, and finally his own frenzy as he built to climax. His strong fingers dug into her hips as he came, and she took pleasure in his pleasure as he jerked within her, guttural sounds coming from his throat.

He wrapped his arms around her and opened his eyes to look down into hers. "You are something else, woman."

"You're, uh—" she fingered his collarbone and touched a mole that grew next to it "—you're passable yourself." She grinned at his outraged glare, his dropped jaw.

"Passable?" He looked up and addressed the trees.

"The little vixen says I'm *passable*. I wouldn't believe it if I hadn't heard it with my own ears!" Troy got down to the serious business of tickling her while she shrieked.

"Stop! Stop! I didn't mean it," Peggy panted, trying to get away from him.

"Repeat after me—'Troy, you are a sex god.' No, 'Troy, you are *the* sex god!'"

"Aaaaiiieeeee!" she squealed, "stop it, stop it, stop it! Troy, you are the sex god!"

He gave her a momentary breather. "Now say, "'Troy, you are the best I've ever had!'"

She blew out a breath and thumped him in the forehead. "Yo, stupid. You don't have to tickle me to get me to say *that*."

"Oh, yeah?" His chest swelled.

She nodded. "But don't puff up like that and get arrogant, or I'll take it back."

"I'm the best she's ever had," he said to a lizard that darted out from behind a terra-cotta pot on the pool deck. The lizard blinked at him and swelled his little neck. "But that goes without saying. Because of course I am the best there is." He took a bow.

"Puh-lease," said Peggy, rolling her eyes and getting out of the pool. Water dripped off her body and she attempted to wring out her hair. The sun felt wonderful on her naked skin, though she knew she couldn't stay out here long, or she'd become a lobster.

"It's true," said Troy, winking at her. He pushed off from the side of the pool and floated on his back, arms under his head.

"Your big head is getting swollen," she told him, "but your other one doesn't look anywhere near so impressive now…oh, yikes!"

He jumped out of the pool and came after her. Peggy ran, but her legs were no match for his longer ones and he caught her within seconds. She tried to twist away, but he caught her around the waist and threw her over his shoulder, caveman style.

"Hey! Put me down!"

He ignored her and walked over to his jeans, which lay in the grass. He toed them up, fished out his keys and smacked her sharply on the bottom when she pounded a fist into his kidneys.

"Ow!"

"You hit me first. Behave." He unlocked the back door and made his way inside with her, locking it behind him. He deposited her on the kitchen table after sweeping off a couple of stray Cheerios with his arm. "Don't think we're done yet, darlin'."

"We're not? I don't think I can take any more!"

"Then you'd better not make comments about things not being impressive."

She looked between his legs. *Oh, my.* "What, do you have a helium pump or something? Where the hell did that come from?" His cock jutted at her, ready for business. "I guess you, uh, never used steroids."

"I wouldn't touch that stuff."

She shrugged.

"Not with a ten-foot pole."

She looked at his pole and smirked. "You men are such exaggerators. That's not ten feet and you know it."

"You've got a real mouth on you, Peggy-Sue," he said, shaking his head. But he laughed. "Now, why'd you ask me about steroids? Was that another charming habit of your fiancé's?"

She nodded.

"So he gave you a CZ *and* you didn't get much action? What did you do, go to www.Losers.com and order one up special?"

Peggy choked. "Something like that."

"Well, I hope they didn't charge you too much. Now, you just lie back and let Uncle Troy and his assistant give you a little massage. It's your turn today."

Uncle Troy's assistant turned out to be a plastic squeeze bottle of honey, shaped like a bear. He liked to sit in the microwave for short periods of time, during which he got all warm and gooey.

Then he liked to be squeezed so that honey ran all over her breasts, at which point Troy had to step in and clean up the mess. With his tongue and a lot of suction. Peggy went ahead and let Uncle Troy and his assistant have their way.

But she also insisted on returning the favor, taking his erection into her mouthful of warm honey and doing a little torturing of her own. It wasn't her favorite thing in the world, but she loved the power she had over him as her lips slid up and down, and his eyes closed and his fists clenched on his knees. He groaned and murmured her name and opened his fists to bury his hands in her hair and stroke the back of her neck.

Finally he pulled her up so that she straddled him and sank down onto him. Her breasts rubbed against the rough hair of his chest, and he took them into his hands, squeezing gently, playing her nipples with his thumbs. The rhythm he set this time was slow, languorous and sweet. He kissed and caressed her, stroking gently with hands, tongue and cock until orgasm rolled over her unexpectedly and she relaxed into bliss.

He gave one last thrust, pulling her bottom down hard, trying to wrest every last iota of pleasure from their lovemaking, while she collapsed onto his shoulder and breathed in his scent. She could get far too used to this.

Peggy sat up at the alarming thought, twisting her hair into a wet knot on the top of her head. Troy's eyes were closed and he was still embedded in her, his hands still warm on her skin.

What exactly did she think she was doing? What had happened to her year alone? And impulse control? And finding a mind-body-spirit balance? Just when she'd decided to devote herself to things like inner peace and aromatherapy and even a little meditation, along came a hot man and she forgot about herself and her personal goals to focus on him. Were women genetically programmed to do this? Screw up their lives in the hopes of a little…pollination?

I am not screwing up my life. Just because I've had a few sexual encounters with this man doesn't mean I've signed over my life to him! And he's an ex-football player, for God's sake. Unmarried for a reason—he likes to play the field.

"What's the matter, Peggy-Sue?" Troy asked the question lazily.

"It's just Peggy." Her tone was sharper than she'd intended for it to be.

"O-kay. What's wrong then, Just Peggy? You starting to obsess again about the powder-puff team being eliminated?"

Actually, she was horrified that it had flitted out of her mind so completely. "Yes. We can't let them do this!"

Troy sighed.

"Don't just sit there, Barrington, like it's a done deal. If enough of us go and raise a ruckus, we can change their minds." She slid off his lap and paced across the kitchen.

"Peggy, stop for a minute. Please understand that I am not trying—not for a second—to minimize the importance of girls playing sports. Softball, soccer, volleyball, basketball—those are great for girls. But football? You and I both know that it's different, even if you don't want to admit that."

Her heart stopped. "What do you mean, Troy?" she asked carefully.

He passed a hand over his face. "Look, I know you're going to get pissed at me for saying this, but football is a contact sport. And maybe girls are bigger and more agile than boys at this age, ten to twelve, but within two or three years that's no longer true. What's the future for a female player then? Getting mowed down by a guy twice her body weight? I'm sorry, but no amount of skill or determination is going to change that."

Peggy tried to control her instant rage, but it didn't do much good. "I just slept with Cro-Magnon man! I don't believe this!"

"Why does speaking the truth make me primitive? Why?"

"Because your truth is slanted and ridiculous and shortsighted! First of all, a quarterback or a kicker or a cornerback doesn't have to have the same body weight as an offensive lineman, and you know it."

Troy snorted. "Kicker is one thing. But the day you have a female quarterback on a mixed team is the day they ice-skate in hell."

"Oh, really? Would that be why there are female fighter pilots, female boxers, a female secretary of state?"

"When was the last time you saw a secretary of state running for her life from someone that outweighs her by 150 pounds, bench-presses three times her weight and runs a 4.7 forty? And now, your pro quarterbacks— and hell, even division one quarterbacks—are at least six-two and weigh minimum 215 pounds. They have to—in order to withstand the beatings they take at the hands of these gigantic linemen and linebackers!

"For Christ's sake, Peggy, I'm not arguing that women aren't competent or lack commitment. I'm arguing that physically most women just don't have the stature to take the step to the next level. And even if that wasn't true, the male culture of football, as a sport, would never accept a female quarterback."

"And that male culture is exactly what needs to change, damn it!" Peggy whirled and kicked one of his kitchen cabinets.

"Hey!"

"*Rat-bastard* male culture! No, it won't ever change, will it? I should know." She kicked the cabinet door again, succeeding in splintering it down the middle panel.

"*Hey!*" Troy was up and gripping her arm now. "Get ahold of yourself. I don't care about the cabinets—I'll be replacing them, anyway—but you're out of control."

"Let *go* of me."

He took a step back and raised his hands, palm out.

She dropped her hands to her thighs and leaned on them, trying not to hyperventilate.

"Where is all this rage coming from, Peg? What did you mean, when you said that you should know?"

She didn't answer. She didn't want to bare her soul to him, and she didn't want to be physically naked in front of him any longer, either. She stalked to the kitchen door and wrenched it open, emerging into the hot sun to get her clothes.

"Peggy? Answer me." He'd followed.

"I don't have to answer to you."

"No, you don't. But you're upset and I'm concerned about you and I wish you would talk to me."

She pulled her skirt on, then her panties, bra and top—all with her back to him. She hunted for her shoes.

"Peggy, why did you leave your college team? It had nothing to do with your official statement, did it?"

For some reason, dread grew inside him. This girl wasn't a quitter. Whatever her reasons had been for leaving the team, they had to have been big.

13

SHE SPUN AROUND to face Troy again. "How the hell do you know what my official statement was?"

"I own a computer. I know how to log on to the Internet. It's pretty rare for a woman to be a starter on a college football team."

"You went snooping."

"I was interested in you. If you call pulling up a newspaper article snooping, then so be it. I pulled up your biography and stats on the Bryce University Web site and then clicked on a link to an article. So sue me."

She jammed one foot into a shoe, then the other.

"The article said you left the team to focus on your studies. That's not true, is it? Peggy…your anger today…" He hesitated. "Were you raped?"

All her blood seemed to rush to her head and pound at her temples. She wrapped her arms around her body as tightly as she could. She shook her head. Then she said slowly, "They tried."

"Jesus," he said. He took a step forward.

"Want to know the gory details?" Peg asked, her voice brittle. "Sure, why not? Three of them got me after practice one day, in a special locker room the university had had to construct just for me. You know, just another pain-in-the-ass aspect of having a girl on the team."

Troy didn't say anything, his gaze boring into hers.

"Anyway, I came out of the shower in a towel just as the door opened and there they were, all three of them. I almost choked on my own spit, I was so scared. I backed into the shower again and grabbed my razor—my Daisy shaver—like I was going to be able to do anything with that." She laughed humorlessly, and Troy winced.

"They crowded into the shower with me and one of them pinned my wrist, razor and all, against the wall. The look on his face… I tried to kick another one in the nuts, but he just grabbed my ankle and wrenched it to the side while he tore off my towel."

"Look, I don't know if I want to hear this—"

"You asked to hear it." Her voice to her own ears was low and deadly.

He shut up, his face half anguished and half furious.

"The one holding my wrist grabbed my breast in his other hand, and the one with my ankle grabbed my crotch. The one in the middle unzipped and pulled out his dick…." Her voice broke.

When she could speak again she continued. "Lucky for me, Coach banged on the door—there was a request for an interview. The three of them froze, and before they could do or say anything I screamed." Peggy swallowed before continuing.

"One of the worst things about it was the delay before

Coach opened the door. Like he'd rather have walked away. Didn't want to see what was behind it...."

Troy cursed and tried to take her in his arms but she backed away from him.

"Coach came in and there I was on the shower floor sobbing, and the one guy was stuffing his dick back into his pants. And all he said to them was, 'Get out.' He turned his back and told me to get dressed and that he would wait for me outside and then we needed to talk.

"We walked to his office and he shut the door and asked me if I was okay. I nodded, and he started to explain how a girl on a football team, no matter how good, was like a woman on a ship—just plain bad luck.

"He said he felt about me like he felt about his own daughters, but he was advising me to leave the team and not to say anything. That I would create a huge scandal, jeopardize not only the team but my own reputation— since they'd say I was a whore who invited them to pull a train on me—and that I'd also endanger his job.

"And he pointed out that I wouldn't be doing anything to advance women in athletics, either. He emphasized the fact that I *hadn't* actually been raped, no matter what their intent. He patted my knee and told me I was a good kid." Peggy took a breath.

"I was so grateful for his kindness to me that I didn't think about being furious at his selfishness. I didn't think about the fact that those creeps had probably done this before or might do it again.

"The only thing in my mind at the time—besides relief and fury—was so dumb. Embarrassment that they had seen me naked. Coach had seen me naked, and how could I ever look him in the face again? There was no way I could play again after that."

"Jesus," Troy said, voice hoarse. He stood there without saying anything for a long time. "So…you never told anyone?"

She shook her head. "Not even my mother. I just wanted to put it out of my mind, bury it, pretend it didn't happen. I figured that if I didn't talk about it, then it would just go away."

"You didn't talk to a counselor or something?"

"No. What good would that have done?"

"It might have helped you deal with what happened!"

She looked at him levelly. "Would you have gone?"

He blew out a breath. "It never would have happened to me."

"But if it had, would you have gone?"

Slowly he shook his head.

"Well, there you go. Neither did I."

"Peggy—" he scrubbed his hands over his face "—I don't know what to say except that I'm so sorry. What you went through was awful. Now I understand why you got so mad in there…." Troy pulled on his own jeans and shoved his hands into his pockets.

She looked at him miserably. "What I don't get is why I inspired so much hatred and contempt, when all I wanted to do was play. It wasn't just those three who were bad—every other player at Bryce University hated my guts. *Why?*

"Not because I had no talent. Not because I was a

horrible person with a bad attitude. Just because I had tits. I cost a *serious* player a spot. A guy. I made the players a laughingstock on the college ball circuit, because they were obviously such 'pussies' that a girl could make the team."

Troy closed his eyes. "The male ego is a complicated thing. Men do incredibly stupid things because of pride."

"Oh, it was *pride* that made them goose me any chance they got? Harass me, come on to me, expose themselves to me? I have another word for it."

"Not every guy could have treated you that way."

"Nah. There were some who just ignored me."

"And maybe on a different campus, in a different group of guys, things would have been different. Not all football players are like that."

"Yeah," she said bitterly. "Whatever."

"You got a lot of press as the only woman starting for the team. Were they jealous of that?"

She shrugged. "Could have been."

He nodded. "I think it must have irritated them."

They stood in silence for a long moment. Then he touched her arm. "C'mon, it's hot out here. Let's go inside. You want something to drink?"

She was parched. "Yeah. But then I need to go. And I *am* going to lodge a protest with the school about their decision. It's just bs."

She followed him inside and let him get a glass of ice water for her, which she gulped down without a lot of grace.

Troy watched her. "Can I ask you something? And

don't get mad. It's just a question, because I really don't understand."

She nodded.

"If that was your experience, then why do you want to keep training girls like my nieces, keep encouraging them to think that maybe one day they can be on a high school or college ball team? Why would you want anyone else to go through what you did?"

Peggy set her cup down with a snap. "Because it's the only way that the system will be challenged and the only hope that someday it will change!"

He folded his arms. "Look, you don't have coed basketball, or coed soccer or anything else. Why should there be coed football? Nobody wants it. The best you could hope for is a women's team."

"Then give us women's teams. But we're not going to get them if we're wiped out at the first scheduling problem or budget cut! I'm asking you to stand with me on this, Troy. Not because you owe me anything, but because you owe your nieces."

He gave her a long, hard stare. Then he looked at the floor. Finally he said, "All right."

Even though she'd demanded it, he could tell she didn't expect his cooperation. Somehow, even though she'd told him her story, she'd lumped him in with the rest of the players who'd hurt her: big, male and unfair.

So Peggy stared at him, a smile of warmth and fond disbelief and gratitude slowly dawning across her freckled face. "Yeah...?"

Something inside him cracked at the sight. He cupped her face in his hands and leaned forward to kiss her lips. "Yeah."

TROY WATCHED HER DRIVE AWAY in her ridiculously cute munchkin-mobile. She herself was ridiculously cute. She didn't look like the kind of woman who had scars or worries; she looked like the all-American girl. Freckles, adorable little upturned nose, big blue eyes.

He thought about three thugs—her fellow ball players—attacking her in a shower stall and wanted to be sick. Team spirit took on a whole new sinister dimension. They'd gone as a posse to rape the little upstart, show her who was boss.

Troy threw the contents of his glass into the kitchen sink and stared down the black hole of the disposal. He whirled and splintered the same cabinet door that Peggy had kicked. It didn't matter, since he'd be gutting the whole damn kitchen within weeks, anyway.

Fury at three unknown men pulsed through him; he knew a desire to pound their faces into pulp, hear the sickening sounds of their bones cracking. The potential for extreme violence shooting through his body and psyche scared him.

He'd managed to stay calm when removing Sam's derelict husband from her house, and that had been tough—but last night's situation came nowhere near the sheer rage that consumed him right now.

The creep punched holes in walls and created scary scenes. But as far as Troy knew, he'd never tried to gang rape a defenseless girl.

Troy began to systematically destroy every cabinet door in his entire kitchen with his bare feet and fists.

The cheap wood and laminate splintered, screws popping loose and veneers peeling back. The old hinges didn't stand a chance of holding up under his assault, nor did the thin panels in the middle of the frames.

When he was done both the room and he were a mess. He got a hold of himself and stared around the shambles, feeling no better than Sam's ex, who'd only kicked in the bottom of one door.

Troy rinsed off his bloody knuckles under the tap and grabbed for the roll of paper towels. At least the cabinet doors hid only dated pots and pans, not a frightened woman and her crying children.

Troy headed for the bathroom off the master bedroom, sat on the edge of the bathtub and poured hydrogen peroxide over his feet. "You are one stupid sonuvabitch," he said aloud, looking at the scrapes, bruises and abrasions. They were evidence of something even stupider: he'd gone and developed feelings for Peggy Underwood, and they were more than guilt feelings for sneaking around trying to break her business's lease.

He told the feelings—whatever the hell they were— to get lost, but he knew it was a losing battle. He thought about the times he'd been a little rough with her sexually, and was deeply ashamed. He weighed twice what she did. How could he have not been gentler?

And where the hell did he go with her from here? No wonder she'd once told him that she wouldn't date him.

I don't date football players. Not ever. He recalled her saying that.

A wave of protectiveness washed over him, and as he sat in the tub and watched the cuts on his feet bleed, he resolved that no matter what happened between him and Peggy in the end, he was going to change her viewpoint on football players. He could help heal some of the wounds of her past.

14

PEGGY DROVE HOME half appalled and half relieved that she'd finally told her story to someone. She wasn't sure why she'd spilled her guts to Troy, but his smug comment about the male culture of football had enraged her. She'd had to make him see that it wasn't okay, the whole boys-will-be-boys mentality.

It was fine for boys to be boys—as long as boys being boys didn't involve them acting like animals.

She started to cry as she drove and hated herself for it, for being weak. But the tears came faster as she thought about her father's reaction to her making the college team. He'd congratulated her, but he'd been puzzled, just like everyone else, as to why she'd wanted to play. She was a girl. The question hung in the air between them, never asked by him and never answered by her.

He'd never connected it to her wanting his attention, never realized that she'd tried to impress him and show him she was just as worthy of his love as that jerk Alan, who had his own dad anyway, and didn't need to take hers, too.

Her mom had flown in for one of the early games, which was sweet, if a little embarrassing. Mom had dressed from head to toe in chartreuse—even her socks—and worn what Peggy could only describe as a Peter Pan hat with a tiny green feather. She'd also brought a set of ancient red-and-white pep-squad pompoms, and cheered in rhyme from the bleachers, looking like a demented Santa's helper.

Peg had wanted to punt her to the North Pole but felt horribly guilty about it. At least one of her parents cared enough to show up—even if it was the one who a) couldn't really afford the plane ticket, and b) didn't know the difference between a field goal and a point after touchdown.

She slicked the tears off her cheeks with the heel of her hand and pulled into her apartment complex, parking the Mini as close to her door as she could. Then she went inside, glanced at Marly's mural and sprawled on the carpet in front of it. The girl she'd painted was full of power and energy and love of life, everything that Peggy had believed in back then and still believed in now. The reason that she coached the powder-puff team. Because girls should have all of those qualities.

Lots of girls dreamed of being cheerleaders, and that was great. But the ones who dreamed of being part of the action on the field should be able to make it happen, too. All it did was expand their possibilities and their freedom to make choices.

Maybe Barrington was right, and the day a coed team accepted a female quarterback was the day they ice-skated in hell. Peggy considered that a whole different issue. Her girls shouldn't have to put up with what she'd experienced. But that was a bridge they'd cross when they came to it. For right now, Peg would concentrate on step one: making sure a female team could exist, with a female quarterback, and without mockery or stereotypes.

Peggy got up, showered and made some calls.

The school had been careful in selecting the teams to be terminated. They weren't all girls: the boys' lacrosse team had been cut in addition to the girls' softball and powder-puff football teams. Field hockey hadn't been cut, just moved inside to the gym.

Peggy decided to be proactive before confronting school officials: better to find an alternative practice area first. The problem was that downtown Miami wasn't exactly full of open, grassy fields.

She'd driven by a couple of areas with signs listing development companies, so she called those first. One guy laughed in her face; the other politely told her that building would commence in ten days and even if it didn't, the liability issues were too overwhelming.

Stymied, she didn't know whether to get into the Mini again and drive around, looking for other areas—or call the parks and rec department, maybe even a real estate agent who wouldn't mind devoting an hour of his or her time to charity.

Across the apartment complex, Peggy saw a sweet-looking older woman locking her door. She wore a powder-blue suit and stockings in the heat, with cream T-strap summer shoes and a matching handbag. She looked as if she were going to church.

Church! Why hadn't Peg thought of it before? There

was a large Catholic church near the school, on a significant parcel of property. Maybe they could get permission to use the church grounds for practice and games.

She herself wasn't Catholic, and didn't want to think about how long it had been since she'd last sat in a pew on a Sunday, but maybe Troy and his family were, or one of the other girls on her puff team. Yes, now that she thought about it, Angela Flores belonged to that very church: there was a bumper sticker on her mother's Range Rover.

Peggy jumped up and went to rummage in her tote for her Palm Pilot. She found it and called Angela's home number.

"Hello, Mrs. Flores? This is Peggy Underwood…."

A WEEK LATER Troy joined Peggy, Sam, Derek, Danni and Laura at the Woodward School to make their case for the team. Mrs. Flores and another girl's father came, too, with their children.

Peggy had gotten the appointment with difficulty, having to call three times and then go in person to secure it from the principal's secretary. It was due to her making a pest of herself that they got a time slot at all. But Peg didn't care if the school thought she was irritating— this was important.

The principal, a harried, ginger-haired woman named Mrs. DeMarco, extended only the barest courtesy as Peg introduced herself and the others. She looked at her watch. She capped her pen and folded her hands on the legal pad in front of her, as if willing them to go away.

Peggy began in a low-key manner and built her case

systematically, bolstered by Troy's support and the expectations of the rest. "In the fifth and sixth grades, as a tomboy, I learned to play football along with boys who were my friends. I had an aptitude for it and a love of the game that brought me freedom and a sense of power and a feeling that I could do anything in the world, after driving the length of the field and scoring a touchdown."

Mrs. DeMarco's polite expression didn't change.

"That feeling continued in junior high and even high school, when I didn't allow gender stereotypes to force me out of a traditionally all-male sport. Much as you didn't allow them, Mrs. DeMarco, to stop *you* from pursuing a graduate degree in education, or dissuade you from taking the steps along your career until you became principal of the Woodward School. Who knows, you may become head of the school board next, or even a congresswoman. The point is, you kept pushing the boundaries for women. And you still do. I admire that, Mrs. DeMarco, and I ask that you foster the same courage in your female students at Woodward."

Aha, the woman was now paying more attention. Peggy forged ahead.

"A girl who has faced down a team of opponents who outweigh and possibly outplay her, a girl who uses her brains and skill to bypass those opponents and show them she's a worthy adversary—those are the girls you need at the Woodward School.

"Football is not an average girl's pastime, not considered a feminine sport. But as long as there is interest in it, how can you deny a girls' team the chance to develop?

Hone their skills? Become the next generation of empow-ered women—women who understand what it means to stand and fight on the same playing field as men?

"Mrs. DeMarco, I do understand Woodward's dilem-ma about time slots at the Coral Gables Youth Center. But if I were to tell you that we have come up with an alternative practice field and host field for games, would you and the advisory board reconsider your position on the powder-puff football team—and the other teams who are being affected in this situation?"

The principal cleared her throat. "Miss Underwood, while I appreciate your heartfelt appeal, the Woodward board reached its decision only after considerable thought and research into the alternatives…."

"We understand that. And we do appreciate the effort that was put into the process. But we're not asking that any further time or energy be expended by the board. All we're asking for is a rubber stamp. We've done the legwork, found a host field, gathered the paperwork—" Peg broke off, and turned to her supporters. "Can the girls themselves show you what the powder-puff pro-gram has meant to them?"

Mrs. DeMarco nodded.

Danni and Laura had brought a scrapbook that they kept, full of pictures and journal entries about what the team meant to them. They took it forward and placed it in front of her, flipping through pages and explaining every photo, while the principal's face began to soften.

Angela Flores stood up and told Mrs. DeMarco that she was going to be president one day, but she'd like to train by being quarterback first. "I'm gonna be ten times as good as Tom Brady," she declared. "And they're gonna put me on the covers of magazines." The principal actually smiled at that.

Peg watched the little girls in action, feeling something expand and unfurl inside her. She'd spurred them to stand up for themselves, to question and work for change. She was a role model for these young women. And that made everything she'd gone through in the past worthwhile, if not okay.

She exchanged a glance with Troy, who stood silent with Derek in his support role, an enigmatic expression on his face. He probably wasn't used to standing in the background.

Finally Peggy and Mrs. Flores handed the principal a letter signed by Monsignor Salas, stating that the church would be pleased to host the team's practices and occasional games until the school's athletic fields were operational again.

The capper was that Peg had arranged for the girls' softball team and the boy's lacrosse team to be able to practice and play there, too. In the face of their determination and organization, the principal had little choice: she announced that the programs would remain active for the year. Secretly she looked pleased.

Whoops from the girls echoed throughout the hall, and Laura even turned a backflip.

A wide grin spread over Troy's face, and after he'd ruffled his nieces' hair, he wrapped Peggy in a bear hug. "Congratulations, Peggy-Sue!"

"Thanks," she said against his shoulder, just as relieved and happy as Danni and Laura. They'd done it! They'd saved the team. "All it took was a little girl power."

TROY'S CHEST HAD TIGHTENED with an unfamiliar emotion. He wasn't quite sure what it was, but he thought it might be pride. He was impressed by Peggy...but the admiration had definitely crossed the line into something more personal.

"Tell you what," he whispered in her ear. "I know how much this means to you. So why don't I take you for some champagne later?" The words were out of his mouth before he remembered that he had to talk to her, had to come clean.

Guilt racked him again. He'd gotten to know her and been intimate with her under utterly false pretences. And what happened now? He was fairly sure that they'd pinpointed After Hours on some code violations. But if he acted to break the lease, he could kiss his relationship with Peggy goodbye.

On the other hand, if he didn't act to break the lease, he could kiss off his dream of a sports hangout and retail store. Sure, he could put it in another location, but it just didn't make sense to pay Coral-Gables-level rent when he didn't have to. And the After Hours location was perfect....

Troy tried to delude himself that maybe if he came clean with Peggy, he could salvage the situation. And confessing would be a lot easier midway through a bottle of Dom or Moët.

"I never turn down champagne," she said with a big grin.

You would if only you knew you were sharing it with a liar and a jerk. But of course he didn't say it aloud—not yet. "I know this place with desserts to die for. They have a twelve-layer chocolate cake—"

"Twelve layers? *Twelve?*"

He nodded.

"When are you picking me up? Or shall we just go now? Can I live in their kitchen for the rest of my life?"

What if you lived in mine for the rest of your life? He almost lost his voice at the thought. He cleared his throat. "You might get awfully round."

"Yeah, but I'd die happy." She frowned as she took in the cuts, bruises and abrasions on his hands for the first time. "Oh, my God! What did you do?"

"Nothing," he said, uncomfortable. "Some, uh, lumber fell." She started to ask him more questions, but the girls ran up and provided a much-needed distraction.

Danni and Laura looked up at him and Peggy. "Uncle Troy? Is Coach your girlfriend?"

"Uh…" Startled, his gaze flew to Peg's.

"No," she replied for him.

At the same time he said, "Kind of."

Danni and Laura's brows knit. "Kind of no?"

How do I handle this one? "Well, I'd like her to be," he said. "But I'm not sure how she feels about it."

They turned to Peggy. "Don't you want to be Uncle Troy's girlfriend?"

Her mouth opened and closed. "I...well, I'd like to be Uncle Troy's *friend*. How's that?"

Laura blurted, "Do you kiss him?"

He was amused to see Peggy's face turn bright red. "No!"

He sent a mocking glance her way, one that clearly said, "Liar."

"Well, if you want to, we won't get mad or anything. Uncle Troy is a hunk. We heard Kimmie's mom say so."

Now it was his turn to flush, while Peggy smirked. "A hunk, huh?"

"I mean," Danni said judiciously, "he's not as cute as Ashton Kutcher, but we think he's pretty cute for an old guy."

This time Peggy laughed out loud.

"Hey!" said Troy. "I'm not an old guy."

"You're pretty old," Laura said, merciless.

"Is that so? Well, see if I work with you on your spirals anymore, young lady."

"That's okay. Coach helps us with that, anyway."

Frustrated, Troy exchanged a glance with Peggy.

They all walked out together, and Sam herded the kids toward her car.

"How's your sister doing?" Peggy asked him quietly. "Has she had any more after-midnight visits?"

He shook his head. "No. I think she'll be undisturbed for a while. When the creep came back to get his truck, we had a chat. I told him I'd pay for a rehab program for him and line him up with a job afterward if he'd sign something to the effect that he won't go near her or the kids until he's cleaned up."

"And he actually agreed to that?"

Troy nodded. "He's basically desperate. Turns out he disappeared like he did because he'd lost his job. He knows he's got a problem, and he knows he can't handle it on his own."

"How are Derek and the girls handling things?"

"They're doing okay. Sam and I are taking them to a family counselor to talk about some issues."

Peggy nodded. Then she looked down at the pavement and traced her toe around a pothole in the parking lot, with all the finesse of the middle school kids she coached. "So, um, what did you mean back there, when you said you'd like me to, uh…"

"Be my girlfriend?"

"Yeah, that."

"Well, here's the deal. You're not the ugliest woman I've ever skinny-dipped with. And when you're not destroying my kitchen cabinets—"

"I'm really sorry about that," she broke in.

Oh, honey, if you only knew how I left them.

"—you have quite a winning personality. So I was thinking that maybe you'd like to try out for the position?"

Her eyes flashed. "*Try out for the position?* Of your *girlfriend?*"

He started to laugh.

"Of all the smug, arrogant—" she hauled off and slugged him in the arm "—butt-heads in the state of Florida, you take the cake!"

He rubbed at his arm. "Ow! But I'm offering to *share* the cake, all twelve layers of it, with *you*. And besides, I'm kidding. I just haven't had a girlfriend in years, so I don't really know how to go about officially acquiring one. Wanna coach me on this, Coach?"

She sputtered.

"What, you don't want to share my cake?"

"I didn't say that."

"Then you'll be my little groupie? My number-one fan?"

"I didn't say that, either!"

"My girlfriend, then. Friend who is a girl. And a really hot kisser."

She glared at him. "Pick me up at seven. We can discuss this after the twelve-layer chocolate cake."

"Jeez," he complained. "I used to have women chasing me. Now I have to bribe one with dessert to even talk to me. I guess my niece is right—I'm getting old."

What he didn't say, as he walked back to the Lotus, was that her hesitation bothered him a great deal.

"What's not to like?" he asked his reflection in the rearview mirror. *Blond hair, blue eyes, one and a half dimples. Chicks dig me—especially when I'm laboring behind the scenes to kick them out of their workplaces. That's my most charming quality—that I'm a lying sack of shit.*

Troy banged his head on the Lotus's steering wheel, because he suddenly realized that he wasn't going to confess his ulterior motives to Peggy after all. He planned to bury them and never dig them up again. Why?

Because there was no way in hell that he could go through with his plan, not now. He'd better start scoping out other locations for his little slice of sports heaven.

He gazed down at the bulge in his pants. "You stupid pecker-head. You are going to cost me tens of thousands of dollars in rent somewhere, just because you had to go spelunking where you didn't belong!"

15

TROY BARRINGTON'S girlfriend. Peggy gulped as she looked into her bathroom mirror and dotted concealer under her eyes. *Girlfriend.* She hated that word.

What *had* happened to a year alone? To finding her inner harmony and expanding her soul and achieving that balance between mind, body and spirit?

Did she really want to be somebody's girlfriend again? Trade in her independence for coupledom and all that it entailed?

Someone to talk to at night. That was a nice thought.

Uh-huh. Meaning someone to argue with about what's for dinner, and whether or not it should be crispier or spicier or saltier or hotter.

Someone to cuddle up to in bed: a definite plus.

Uh-huh. Meaning someone to leave the toilet seat up so you fall in with a splash at night.

Someone to have fantastic sex with! How can you argue with that?

Uh-huh. Meaning someone who will eventually forget the definition of the word foreplay *and roll you into the wet spot when he's done.*

Peggy shuddered. And then there'd be the endless games and expectations....

Will I have to shave my legs every single day? Is he a TV addict, with ESPN being a third wheel in the relationship? And oh, the horror! Has he got a nose like a bloodhound, able to track my secret stash of chocolate chip cookies and consume them within seconds?

The possibilities—no, probabilities—got worse the more she thought about it.

Does he have possessive guy buddies who will plot my imminent demise? What is his attitude toward money? Will he expect me to do his laundry?

Can I really see myself living with this man for the rest of my life, or would I rather he drove his car into the lake tomorrow? Will he pop the question this month/holiday/year? What's his mother like, and could I handle seeing her nappy head on my guest-room pillow for two weeks per year? Beyond the mother, does he have psychotic relatives? Could I handle their *nappy heads on my guest-room pillows?*

"Noooooooooo," Peggy moaned aloud. She stopped putting on makeup immediately, not bothering with any at all on her eyes. Instead of blowing her hair dry and leaving it loose in silky waves, she scraped it back wet, into a ponytail. She even thought about spraying Raid on her throat instead of perfume.

Girlfriend? She'd rather be eaten slowly by a twelve-foot alligator.

And then there was the fact that Barrington was a football player. What in the hell had she been thinking? Not that he was in any way responsible for her past, but did she need to be reminded of it every single day? Coaching little girls in pink jerseys was one thing. Dating a former strong safety was another....

She pulled some ugly cargo pants out of her closet and paired them with a baggy T-shirt and ancient Converse high-tops. There, that looked completely inappropriate for some fancy dessert place and quaffing champagne. Perfect. And for an evening bag, she'd shrug on a backpack. Now *where* had she put the Raid?

TROY ADJUSTED his silk tie and wiggled the toes of his left foot a little in their Italian lace-ups. The tie was overkill—nobody wore ties in South Florida—but he wanted to make an impression. Peggy was worth it.

And if he was finally going to relinquish his freedom and become someone's boyfriend—God, what a weird word! He wasn't a boy and he wasn't her friend, because in his book, friends didn't want to screw each other's brains out—then he felt that he should do it in style.

He raised his hand and knocked on her apartment door. When she opened it, he blinked.

"Hey, tiger," she said. "Nice tie." And she tugged on it, before turning quickly and whacking him in the chest with...a backpack? She locked the door and shot him a grin.

Where the hell did she think they were going? The South American jungle? He peered down at her. She'd scraped her hair back into a horrifically unattractive style and it looked greasy. She wore no makeup that he could see, and had dark smudges under her eyes.

Troy drew his eyebrows together. The thing was, she didn't look at all tired. In fact she seemed downright perky. And somehow determined. Hmm.

What kind of woman dressed this way when a man had promised champagne and dessert? Either a stupid one, or this one. What the hell was she up to?

Peggy had dropped her keys, and now as she bent to get them he looked at her suspiciously. The fading evening light caught her hair and created a golden halo…except for something white and gooey, a small glob, right on the back of her head, near the band holding her hair. It looked like a curd of cottage cheese. With sudden clarity Troy knew what it was. She'd smeared Crisco into her hair.

Crisco.

And the smudges under her eyes were deliberate. Probably made with eye shadow. She also smelled like… Sweet Jesus! Had the woman sprayed Raid onto her T-shirt?

Troy had been out with a lot of females, all of whom had taken pains with their appearance for him. He'd just never been out with one who'd taken *this* tack. Gallantly he offered his arm, trying not to wrinkle his nose at the way she smelled. They descended her apartment stairs.

He unlocked the passenger-side door of the Lotus and he handed her in, silently praying that she hadn't hosed down the back of her shirt with the insecticide, too. He really didn't want his leather seat absorbing the stink.

Troy thought about scrapping his plans to take her to the primo Miami restaurant Azul, where he'd reserved a table overlooking the ocean. And then his sense of humor took over. Two could play at this game.

She'd made herself look deliberately unattractive for him. He suspected that this was due to the whole *girl-friend* conversation earlier in the day. So she didn't want to be his girlfriend? The idea intrigued him, offended him, actually—but he also saw through the bluff. If she truly wasn't interested, she wouldn't be sitting here in his car.

They arrived at the lushly landscaped Mandarin Oriental hotel, overlooking Biscayne Bay. Azul nestled inside. Valet attendants rushed each car that pulled under the spectacular modern portico. Troy had a quiet chuckle as one of them leaped to the passenger side of the Lotus and handed out Combat Girl, the lump of Crisco still intact on her head.

Really, it was that which decided him. He was going to marry Peggy Underwood one day, and never let her forget this utterly seductive outfit.

The poor valet guy let go of her hand, wrinkled his nose and sneezed. Peggy gave him a charming smile and thanked him. Troy propelled her inside the hotel and over to the elevators. They rode up with an elderly couple who also looked as if they didn't enjoy eau de Raid.

The restaurant personified beachfront elegance, with low, intimate lighting and walls of glass putting the ocean and Miami skyline on exhibit. The maître d' blinked once at Peggy's couture de combat and hesitated.

"We have a reservation," Troy said smoothly. "A window table." Casually, he rested his palm on the man's fussy little walnut podium, and let a hundred-dollar bill slide out and down the page of the book. "Barrington." A few years back, he wouldn't have had to bribe their way in, no matter what his date was wearing. How the mighty had fallen.

"Very good, sir," the maître d' said, the bill disappearing into his own palm. "Right this way."

Peggy was the object of many disapproving gazes as they threaded their way through the sophisticated seating and expensive contemporary sculpture. Troy wondered how she'd managed to find pants quite that unflattering. She really must have worked at it, because she had a hot body.

Truth to tell, she still looked beautiful in a sloppy, derelict sort of way. Nothing she did could change the delicate bone structure of her face, or ruin the adorable pug nose, or dim the blue of her eyes.

Troy pulled out her chair, got her settled and sat himself. The air-conditioning wafting over them picked up the insecticide on her and sent it eddying to his nostrils. He coughed into his napkin.

"May I offer you something to drink, sir and madam?" A black-jacketed waiter appeared like a genie out of a bottle.

"Mademoiselle," said Peggy, a little too emphatically in Troy's opinion. Chopped liver, was he?

"Yes, please," he said. "A bottle of Cristal."

"Right away, sir."

Troy placed his napkin in his lap and leaned back expansively. "Don't you look lovely tonight, Peggy."

She raised an eyebrow. "You like this outfit, huh? Sorry, but I was out running errands and I didn't have time to shower and change."

Such a little liar. He could smell the shampoo and soap underneath the Raid. Troy leaned forward. "That turns me on," he said softly. "You know, that our relationship has progressed to the point of casualness. That you don't worry about what you look like in front of me."

A flash of annoyance crossed her face.

Ha. Got ya. "Because," he continued, "when I think about what I want in a girlfriend, it's definitely not fussiness."

She'd definitely blanched at the word *girlfriend.* Wasn't that a kick to a man's ego? So that's what all this was about. She wanted him to back off. Interesting. And ironic, considering that she was the only woman he'd felt like chasing in a damn long time.

Their champagne arrived. He tasted it, pronounced it good, and the waiter filled their glasses. She almost dove into hers, but he raised his glass in a toast.

"To being girlfriend and boyfriend."

She froze. "Heh, heh. Don't you think those terms are so old-fashioned? And somewhat…goofy."

"Goofy?"

"Uh-huh. Let's just drink to great sex. How's that?" She didn't wait for him to answer, just chugged almost half her glass.

His lips twitched. "All right, then. Here's to great

sex." His voice carried farther than hers did, and the elderly couple they'd ridden the elevator with turned to stare. Troy winked at them and drank. Scandalized, they presented their backs.

"Now," he said, once she had set down her glass. "Do you want to tell me why there's Crisco in your hair and gray eye shadow under your eyes? And was it really necessary to shower yourself with insecticide just to repel me?"

She froze for an infinitesimal moment, then recovered, looked him right in the eye and pretended ignorance. "*What?* Have you lost your mind? What kind of woman would do those things?"

"I'm not quite sure what kind of woman does those things, but I *am* quite sure you've done them. Give me credit for some intelligence, Peggy-Sue."

"It's just Peggy," she said tightly. A telltale flush was rising from her chest to her temples. "And how do you know about the Crisco?"

He crooked a finger at her, and she bent her head forward. He removed the glob from her hair and smeared it right onto the tip of her nose.

She sat there for a long moment, gritting her teeth. Then she removed it with her napkin.

The waiter appeared again. "Have you had a chance to look over the menu? Would you care to hear the specials?"

"No thanks," Troy said. "I believe we'd just like two slices of the twelve-layer chocolate cake."

"Very good, sir." The waiter disappeared.

"Now, where were we?" Troy asked. "Oh, right.

Crisco in the hair. So I'm assuming that you brushed your teeth with baking soda, too?"

"Very funny." Peggy upended her champagne glass into her mouth. He poured her some more.

"So what is it, exactly, about the word *girlfriend* that you hate so much?"

"It's not the word, okay? It's just that I made a promise to myself to spend this year alone. To get reacquainted with *me,* however stupid that sounds."

"It doesn't sound stupid."

"I spent all this time trying to make my last relationship work. Trying to fix someone who didn't want to be fixed, and put up with someone I should never have put up with."

"Okay."

"And I vowed that I was going to love, honor and cherish *myself* for a year afterward. So here it is, four months later, and *you* come along."

"I'm so very sorry," he said dryly.

"Hey, I didn't mean it that way…it's just that it's bad timing. I don't want to be anyone's girlfriend right now."

He thought about it. "Well, you said you didn't date football players, either, but you've gone out with me a number of times now. And maybe you should look at all this from a different perspective. Why did you stay with Mr. Limp Dick? He obviously didn't make you very happy."

She fiddled with her silverware and didn't answer.

"I'm gonna make a suggestion, but you probably won't like it. I think you stayed with him because he was safe. He was a loser who didn't challenge you and couldn't violate you. He couldn't do you any harm."

She inhaled sharply and refused to look at him.

"After all those years of toughing it out, and then the fear and disgust of the men you played football with, you chose someone on the opposite end of the spectrum. Someone safe. And if I had to make a guess, I'd say that your feelings were never that engaged."

"That's not true!" Her eyes blazed, and he knew he'd hit pay dirt. He was dead-on.

"Whatever you say. But you just think about it. You chose a guy who fulfilled all your expectations of men at that point—somebody who'd disappoint you on every level. He was *safe,* Peggy. But he sure as hell didn't help you move on."

She'd pulled her hands back into her lap now, and he'd bet they were clenched and white-knuckled. Her face was shuttered and grim.

"He didn't help you, and in fact he probably did even more damage. But that's all I'm going to say. I'll just ask you to think about it. Think about why the word *girlfriend* bothers you so much. Is it the word, Peggy? Or is it the idea of intimacy?"

She took a deep breath. "Don't be ridiculous, Troy. It's the word. I hate the word."

Troy nodded. "Okay, fair enough." He'd pushed as hard as he could. It was time to backtrack to humor and lighten the atmosphere. "Then I have a suggestion—we scrap the word *girlfriend* completely. Why don't we call you my chick instead? Or my ho? Would that help?"

She sputtered over her ice water, the expression on her face comic.

He just grinned at her. "Solves everything, doesn't it?"

She looked at him darkly. "You know, if they weren't about to bring me chocolate cake—twelve-layer chocolate cake—I wouldn't put up with this. I'd leave right now."

"What about the champagne?"

"Oh, I'd take that with me."

"That is *so* cold."

"Mmm, isn't it?" She lounged back in her chair and took another sip. "But then I wouldn't have to share it."

"Aw, come on. Champagne is the one drink in the world that you cannot have alone. It's like a law—you have to share it with someone."

"Even someone whom you strongly dislike? Someone who—"

"Is still sitting here with you in public, even though you're dressed like Rambo and smell like a dead cockroach?"

She glared at him.

"Yes, I think I'm exactly the kind of guy you should share your champagne with. One who's tolerant of madwomen."

She actually pushed out her chair this time and made it halfway out of her seat.

"Cake for madam?" The waiter appeared behind her.

Troy watched her struggle, delighted. She eyed the door with longing. She eyed the cake with longing. She eyed him with something close to hatred. But the chocolate cake won the battle.

"Mademoiselle," she hissed, and sat down again. "Thank you."

The waiter nodded and set the cake in front of her. He sniffed the air with a puzzled expression. Then he set Troy's cake down, noted their drained glasses and picked up the Cristal bottle, which was now empty.

"Another, please," said Troy with a nod.

Peggy put a forkful of cake into her mouth, and the sudden change in her expression was almost comic. Ecstasy, bliss, euphoria: all of these words summed it up. Her eyes almost rolled up into her head.

"It is good, isn't it?" He smiled at her.

"Only for this cake would I remain sitting with someone who suggests that the term *ho* is a pleasing alternative to *girlfriend*."

"I think you know I was kidding."

The waiter appeared again with the second bottle of Cristal and a scented candle, which he set in the center of the table along with the one already present. He filled their glasses once again.

"Is Raid flammable?" Troy asked. "Because I really think that would be the perfect ending to a romantic evening. My, uh, chick going up in smoke."

"Chick is not an acceptable alternative to the G word either." Peggy forked up another mouthful of cake and blissed out.

"Bed-buddy? Boink-baby? I mean, trust me, there are a lot of terms we could use here, some of them not so nice."

Peggy swallowed. "Troy? Darling Troy?"

"Yeah?"

"If you want to have any prayer of getting laid to-night, would you just shut up?"

"Okay," he said agreeably. He might be chopped liver and mow his own lawn now, but he wasn't stupid.

16

PEGGY GIGGLED and leaned on Troy's arm for support as they walked through the gate of his backyard. Her legs felt like rubber and her head was full of tiny bubbles. She had a strong suspicion that she had a chocolate mustache, but couldn't seem to care enough to lick it off.

Troy stripped off her shirt and threw it into a clump of rose bushes. "Jesus," he said. "You reek."

More giggles attacked her while he unbuttoned and unzipped her cargo pants and pulled off her shoes. The pants landed on the thick ficus hedge surrounding the yard and one of the high-tops flew over it.

He unhooked her bra and stripped off her panties, then picked her up bodily and tossed her into the pool. He waited until she came up sputtering and then instructed her to sit on the steps. "You're too drunk to swim alone," he said. "Stay there until I get back."

"H'okay," she said agreeably. "Kill you in a lil' bit." She was mad on principle that he'd thrown her in, but the water felt erotic, cool and silky against her naked skin, and she leaned her head against the edge of the pool.

Troy reappeared from inside, now naked himself and

with a bar of soap. She giggled again. "'S pretty big bathtub," she said.

"Yeah. Come here. We're gonna get all that Raid off of you. I still can't believe you sprayed that on your shirt."

"Was gonna hit my neck, but figured it wasn't very good for me."

"No, you little moron, it's not." He lathered up his palms and soaped her torso, paying special attention to her breasts, if truth be told.

"I din' spray *those*."

"Let's pretend you did," said Troy, fondling them with great appreciation.

"H'okay. Mmm, that feels good."

He soaped her rib cage, belly and neck thoroughly, rinsed her by swishing her through the pool, and then repeated the whole process.

"That can't be good for the pool," she said.

He shrugged. "Now come here." He kissed her, shooting more tiny bubbles into her brain, and she smiled against his lips. "Shh. Don' tell anyone, but I like you."

"Enough to be my…never mind." He kept on kissing her, and set her on the first step of the pool while he knelt on the third between her legs. Soon his mouth was on her breasts, sucking and pulling, nipping here and there, gently kneading until she felt almost crazy with desire.

He turned her around, gathering up her still-Crisco-covered hair and kissing her neck, her shoulders, all over. She could feel his erection against her backside, and she opened her thighs, slid it between them as his hands roamed over her body. She wanted him inside her, but he made no move to enter.

He palmed her breasts again, driving her wild with his fingers, nipping her shoulder.

She wiggled her backside against him and finally gave a not-so-subtle nudge when he still didn't take the hint. He laughed, and slipped his hands between her legs. "What do you want, Peggy-Sue?"

"You," she said, pushing against him. The tiny bubbles were popping down there, now, too.

"What part of me?" he asked, nuzzling her ear.

Impatient, she said, "Your big toe! What d'you think?"

"My toe, huh." His chest rumbled against her spine. "First request on that one, honey. I can honestly say that no woman has ever begged me for that."

She reached behind her and grabbed his penis, tugging on it. "That's what I want!"

"Thank you for the clarification." He removed her hand. "But I gotta tell you," he said, his fingers working cleverly to find the little nub between her thighs, "that what you're asking for is now off limits, reserved only for girlfriends. I can't give it to ya, babe."

She started to whimper, half in pleasure and half with frustration. "Barrington, do you even know how much I hate you? Aaaaah!"

"Yeah. As much as I hate you," he said, taking his hand away and fanning cool water against her trouble spot.

"Please," she whispered.

"I do love it when you discover your manners."

"Please."

He thrust into her and she arched her back, quivering. He gave her three strokes before pulling out. "So, are you my girlfriend yet?"

She gritted her teeth.

"Hmm?"

"Just for tonight."

He entered her again, slowly and teasingly. "Nope, you gotta do better than that."

Warmth and fullness spread through her, and a pulse started deep inside. He stroked in and out, and cupped her breasts in his big warm hands again, flicking her nipples with his thumbs.

Then he took his hands away and slipped out of her. "You my girlfriend?"

"Yes," she finally panted, willing to promise anything or be anyone if he would just bring her release. Troy drove into her fast and furious this time, as if he couldn't get far enough inside her.

The warmth and fullness and friction built to a burn, and she burst into flames, shivering from head to toe in hot, helpless convulsions. Troy followed her seconds later, and they collapsed on the steps, water lapping around them.

After washing the Crisco out of her hair, she slept in his bed snuggled against him that night. It was something that girlfriends just *did,* he told her. She shot the finger at him sleepily, and he rolled her into his arms. He threw a big, muscular leg over hers and she felt warm and safe and beyond sated.

He promised to make her pancakes in the morning before she went to work, and they drifted off to sleep.

TROY WOKE HER in the most blissful possible way, and afterward she yawned and stretched like a cat.

"It's just terrible being my girlfriend, isn't it?" he said, yanking on a T-shirt and some shorts. "I mean, look at the abuse you put up with—two orgasms before breakfast."

She stuck her tongue out at him.

"You know, I am more and more impressed by your stunning maturity," said Troy. "I'm still trying to absorb the whole Crisco/Raid combo. That took finesse." He threw one of his T-shirts at her. "Here, you can consider that a perk of your new position as *girlfriend*."

"Ooooh!" She threw it back at him.

"What? Was it something I said? You're not putting on the Raid-rag again, that's for sure." He threw it back at her, and this time she put it on. After all, her other clothes were still outside in the bushes.

She got out of bed and trailed him to the kitchen, where she stood and blinked in shock. "Your *cabinets*. What happened?"

He stopped needling her long enough to look sheepish. "Uh. Me." He hadn't cleaned up; he hadn't been there much. She opened and closed her mouth without saying anything. She shook her head.

"I kind of…finished what you started the other day." He shrugged at her expression. "Girls cry. Guys destroy things. Hey, don't look at me that way. You inspired it! You kicked one first."

She still stood there, speechless. Not a single cabinet door was intact. They were splintered, hinges hanging drunkenly, utterly destroyed. "You were...upset by what I told you?"

"Nah, I was thrilled." He threw up his hands in exasperation. "Of course I was upset! If I had the names and addresses of those guys I'd make sure they looked worse than the cabinets. I don't suppose you'd give me that info, huh?"

"Not a chance." She tried to absorb the fact that Troy hadn't thrown a single punch at his brother-in-law during the whole commotion at Sam's. But he'd done this to his kitchen over something that had happened to her more than ten years ago.

"I didn't think so." He inspected his knuckles and then gestured toward the damage. "I'm remodeling in a few weeks, anyway. So no big deal. Demo has commenced, that's all."

No wonder his feet looked bruised and cut up. His hands, too. Her heart turned over.

"Sorry if you think I'm a caveman. But look on the bright side—I'm a caveman who makes pancakes and bacon! How do you like your bacon? Crunchy or chewy?"

"Chewy."

"Huh. First strike against you. Bacon should only be eaten crunchy. But for you, I'll take some out of the pan early."

"Thanks," she said.

"Mickey Mouse pancakes? Or regular round?"

"Mickey Mouse."

"Excellent choice. I craft *exquisite* ears. Orange juice?"

She nodded. "Where are the cups? I'll get it. By the way, you are way too energetic in the morning."

"Cranky, are we? Even after two orgasms. I suppose you want coffee, too?"

She clasped her hands as if in prayer.

"God, you demanding woman."

"Hey, I'm just settling into my new role as girlfriend. Aren't we supposed to be high maintenance?"

"True. That is generally part of the job description." He grinned at her as he pulled a coffee filter out of a cabinet, popped it into the top of the machine and spooned in coffee. Soon the coffeemaker was gurgling away, the bacon was starting to spit in a pan, and Troy was whipping pancake batter in a bowl.

I could actually get used to this, she thought. *This is really nice.*

"What time do you have to be at the spa?" he asked.

"Not until one. I'm working till closing at midnight tonight."

"So we can have a nice, leisurely breakfast, read some of the paper, maybe skinny-dip a little." He waggled his brows at her.

"Sounds great." She found some clean glasses in the dishwasher and pulled a pitcher of orange juice out of the refrigerator. She poured it and took a sip of hers while Troy, true to his promise, made a perfect Mickey Mouse hotcake on his plug-in griddle.

"Amazing," she said.

But he wasn't done yet. He flipped it and foraged in the fruit drawer of the fridge. When it came out of the pan, he gave Mickey blueberries for eyes, a grape for a nose and a raspberry mouth.

Ridiculous, but when he set the plate in front of her, she teared up. "My dad used to do fun pancakes. He'd pour the batter into these big aluminum cookie cutters my mom had. We had a gingerbread man and a heart and a sun and a crescent moon."

"But you've never had mouse-cakes."

She shook her head and smiled. "Nope. I don't think my Dad could have done it freehand."

"So once again, I am The Man." He held his spatula aloft like a scepter and took a bow for an imaginary adoring crowd.

She rolled her eyes. "Yes, Troy. You are The Man."

The microwave pinged—he'd warmed the syrup in a glass measuring cup—and he got it and set it on the table next to her. Then he brought her some bacon that he'd cooled on a paper towel. "Would madame—excuse me, *mademoiselle*—care for anything else at the moment?"

"Just the pleasure of your company. Thanks."

They ate in companionable silence over the newspaper, after a brief tussle over who got the sports section first. She compromised and took the A section, catching up on world events. She read about another suicide bombing, more unrest in the Middle East, somber economic forecasts. The overnight body count in Miami, always an active city for murders. The typically cheery stuff.

Finally Troy stretched and yawned. "Listen, I'm going to take a shower, okay?"

She nodded.

"You're welcome to join me," he said with a leer.

"I'm really not functional until I've had two cups of coffee. You go ahead."

After retrieving the bar of soap from outside, he disappeared, and she heard the sound of running water. She sipped at her coffee and got absorbed in an article about common household cleaners that contained dangerous carcinogens. Brilliant....

Troy's phone rang, and she debated whether or not to answer it. She decided not to—despite her new, dubious girlfriend status, she still felt like a guest in his house, and he did have an answering machine.

It picked up, and a man's voice boomed into the room. "Troy, buddy. It's Jerry here. Listen, I did some checking around and you are gonna be one happy sonuvabitch, because it turns out that your After Hours place never got a permit to install their whadyacallit— the special tub where they do the mud baths and so on. So you are in luck, they are in violation of the lease, and you can break it. Your sporting goods store should be a reality soon! I'll get going on a notification letter for you, big guy. Later." There was a click as he broke the connection, and then a shrieking silence.

Peggy stared at the machine, almost unable to process what she'd just heard. *You're in luck, they are in violation of the lease, and you can break it. Your sporting goods store is about to become a reality!*

She recalled how odd Troy had been the first time he'd come to After Hours. Looking around the place as if he were an engineer…purchasing a body-treatment package that he clearly wasn't much interested in.

Her blood boiled.

She recalled him choking at Benito's when she'd asked him if he'd found a location for his new store. And all along, she'd been happily oblivious. He'd used her. *Girlfriend?*

More like tool. Mark. Easy recreational lay.

I am so stupid that I redefine the word. I make the whole concept *of stupid look like genius.*

Fury spilled into her veins and she felt sick. She wanted to spew his Mickey Mouse pancakes all over his wreck of a house…the house that she'd come to think of as sweet and charming in its shabbiness. Sweet and charming like him.

She got up to find that her legs were shaking, along with the rest of her body. She thought about hurling her coffee cup through the sliding glass door.

She thought about murdering Troy, *Psycho*-style, in the shower. She thought about boiling his head on the 1930s stove. If she confronted him right now, she wasn't sure she could be responsible for her actions.

Girlfriend. Her temples throbbed. She left her coffee sitting on the newspaper and went outside in search of her pants. She plucked them off the ficus, decided she didn't care about finding her underwear and tracked down one shoe. She vaguely remembered the other one flying over the hedge. To hell with it, too. She scooped up her purse and slammed out the gate of the backyard.

She'd made it to the street when Troy emerged from the front door, the lower half of him wrapped in a towel. "Peggy?"

Slowly she turned and looked at him, taking in the powerful chest and arms, the sunlight catching the water droplets falling from his hair, his puzzled expression.

"You *rat bastard*," she said.

"What?"

"You *pathetic lowlife*."

He took a step toward her. "Peggy?"

"Girlfriend?" she screamed at him, her rage erupting like a geyser between them. "When were you going to tell me, Troy? After you'd explored every sexual position with me?"

"Tell you what?"

"You booked our body-treatment package so that you could get into After Hours and find some bullshit violation! In order to break the lease and kick us out!"

"Jerry. It was Jerry who called, wasn't it?" He scrubbed his hands over his face, and she knew he was guilty.

Some small part of her had wanted him to deny it, still hoped that it wasn't true.

She lost all respect for him and let go a stream of invective. "Unbelievable! And then you had *sex* with me? *Over and over again, while you were planning this the entire time?*"

"It's not like that—"

"It *is* like that! Go listen to your own damn answering machine and tell me it's not true!"

"I wasn't actually going to do it—"

"Save the bullshit for someone else, Barrington. You make me sick!" She turned and walked down the street.

"Where the hell are you going like that? Barefoot? You can't walk home!"

"I can do whatever the hell I please, you asshole."

Troy ran after her, still holding the towel at his waist. "Look, can we talk about this?"

"I have nothing to say to you—"

"Let me at least drive you home, for chrissakes!"

"—except may you rot in hell."

"Peggy, damn it, let me explain!"

"What are you going to explain, huh? That you're a complete dickhead? A liar? An opportunist and a two-faced piece of dog shit?"

"Call me names if it will make you feel better, but let me—"

"Girlfriend!" she shrieked at him.

"That's one I've never been called—" He put a hand on her arm and tried to stop her.

"Get your hands off me!"

He winced and put a hand to his ear. "Message received, loud and clear, thanks."

"So how does this play out now, Troy? Is it *me* who delivers the message to my business partners? Oh, by the way, that guy I've been screwing is the landlord, and now that he's ready to move on, we have to get out! The fifty grand we all borrowed to build out the place and remodel is history, and we may as well default on the loan tomorrow."

"There is no such message to deliver, that's what I'm trying to tell you—"

"Stop lying to me! What, are you going to tell me next that I am such a Grade A lay that you were planning to forfeit all business sense and open your sporting goods store somewhere else?"

"Yes!"

She laughed, and even to her own ears the sound was high and wild. "Don't bother."

"Peggy, what do I have to do—"

"You've done enough. Go screw yourself, Troy." She walked away, desolate and not caring that the hot pavement was burning the soles of her feet. Three blocks east and a couple of turns should bring her to Miracle Mile, where she hoped a bedraggled, barefoot woman could catch a cab. Peggy found her sunglasses in her bag and jammed them onto her nose, protection not only from the sun but from strangers who might see her cry in public.

She half hoped Troy would follow her, but only so she could push him in front of a bus.

17

TROY STARED AFTER PEGGY, her wild red hair streaming down her back, his shirt covering her almost to the knees of her ugly cargo pants. She looked ridiculous, beyond furious and…beautiful.

Why hadn't he had the talk with her when he'd had the chance? If he could have kicked his own ass, he would have.

Instead, he stood stupidly in the middle of his residential street, slowly becoming aware of the fact that his towel was causing a great deal of interest.

Across the street and two doors down, Mrs. Costas was watering her mailbox, staring fixedly at his rear end.

Next door a pair of beady eyes, a hooked nose and a white fluff of hair peered at him from behind the navy blue curtains. Mrs. Zavala looked like a cross between Mata Hari and a pelican. Troy waved at her and hitched up the towel.

Meanwhile down the street the mail delivery truck, driven by a blond woman named Sally, jumped a curb and mowed down two garbage cans. Troy decided that maybe he should go inside before he was kidnapped for salacious purposes by some perverted housewife in a minivan.

He cursed and stalked toward his front door. If he'd been in a better mood, he might have shaken his booty for them all. But unfortunately the one woman he *wanted* to look at him that way was currently hiking home barefoot.

Not to mention the fact that she'd told him to go screw himself. He sighed. Clearly, he wasn't going to break the lease and kick her out of the retail space. But that wasn't enough at this point. How the hell did he get her to talk to him again?

Flowers didn't work. He personally selected them at the florist, handwrote the card and asked that they be delivered to her at After Hours that day.

Peggy wrote, in block letters on a piece of computer paper, Return to Sender. Then she stapled it on securely, through six of the nicest blooms.

Stymied, he tried calling her there, but even Shirlie was cold, and Peggy wouldn't come to the phone.

He tried sitting on her apartment steps when she was due to come home, but when she saw him from the parking lot, she called building security, and he was asked, in no uncertain terms, to leave.

Exasperated, Troy called Jerry in the hopes that legally he could force a tenant to meet with him. Jerry asked him what the hell he was smoking.

Troy even tried to enlist the help of his nieces, Danni and Laura. Borrowing Sam's SUV, he drove them to practice with a gorgeously wrapped two-pound box of

Godiva chocolates. He watched them take it to Peggy, who talked to them for a couple of minutes, then rubbed their backs and kissed them both on the cheek. Interesting.

Troy watched as she walked to the twenty-yard line they'd spray painted in the church's grass, tossed the box up into the air and kicked it clean through the goalposts. Then she sent a glare in his direction and started the girls on their sprints.

All righty, then. That went over well. Annoyed, Troy gunned the engine and drove away, trying to think of some way to get through to her. A few hours later he had it. He was a client of After Hours. A client who had purchased a body-treatment package and paid in full—but hadn't received the second half of the hot stone massage or the last treatment. Legally they had to give him what he'd paid for. Didn't they?

PEGGY WENT TO WORK and football practice even though she felt more like curling up under her covers and not moving for about three weeks. That was what animals did when they were wounded, wasn't it? They crawled into a dark, quiet space and waited for time to heal them.

Too bad she had opposable thumbs, a social security number and no fur. She also had rent to pay and clients to massage and little girls to coach. She couldn't just drop down a hole and off the planet, no matter how much she wanted to.

Her hands were sunk deep into the dough of Pugsy Malloy's back one day when Shirlie knocked on the door. "Peggo? I'm really sorry to disturb you, but I have to talk to you about something."

Peg frowned. It was not cool to interrupt a client's session this way. She placed a hot towel on Malloy's back, covered him with the sheet and a cotton blanket and excused herself with an apology.

"What?" she said. "Shirl, this better be important."

"It is. Troy Barrington called again—"

"I thought you said this was important."

"Listen! This time he is demanding the last part of his body-treatment package. He says he's paid for it and you can't turn him down. He even threatened to sue."

"Oh, he did, did he?" Peggy gritted her teeth while her blood came to a simmer. She thought for a moment. "Fine. You tell Mr. Big Shot to come in Monday night. I will personally oversee his body mistreatment."

Shirlie's eyes widened. "But we're closed on Mondays."

"So? You tell him that's the only time I can work him in. Monday at 7:00 p.m."

"O-kaaaay," said Shirlie. She started to turn away, but then stopped, smirking. "So you never did tell me about his equipment."

Peggy shot her a level look and folded her arms across her chest. "Because it wasn't even worth mentioning. Barrington's got a piece of elbow macaroni down there. Steroids, I'm telling you."

Shirlie blinked in abject disappointment. "God. That's almost *criminal*. Talk about false advertising!"

Peggy went back into the treatment room. Pugsy was

so relaxed that he was almost drooling. She gently removed the towel from his back and worked at finding the musculature under all his padding. His eyelids fluttered and he murmured, "You're the best."

She smiled. Such a sweet man. She applied more oil to her hands and tended to a couple of tight spots in his lower back. Pugsy groaned and moved his hips. He moved them again.

"Are you okay?" she asked. "Does something hurt?"

Pugsy's legs went rigid and he pushed against the table with his hands. His butt quivered. He emitted one small grunt and then lay still.

She froze. Had he…? Oh, *euw.* This was an occasional hazard of the job, but it hadn't happened to her in years, and the fact that it was Pugsy particularly repulsed her.

"I think I pulled my, uh, shoulder the other day," he said in an odd voice.

She found hers and took her cue. "Oh? I'm so sorry to hear that. Why don't we end early today. I'd hate to aggravate that."

"I think that's a good idea."

"All right," she said brightly. "Then I'll just leave you alone to get dressed."

"Yep."

Peggy fled the room and resolved to burn those sheets if her hunch was correct. Unfortunately, it was.

When another elaborate arrangement of exotic flowers arrived for her later in the day, she had a feeling she knew who they were from—and it wasn't Troy. This time, she had the flower guy take them straight to the hospital.

OVER THE NEXT COUPLE of days, Peggy thought a lot about how she should handle her last appointment with Snake-in-the-Grass Barrington. She could a) not speak to him at all, just stick him in the mud bath and maybe toss the spa's tiny color television in after him, b) be sugar sweet and then boil him in the bath like a shellfish, or c) pretend that she'd forgiven him and then get her revenge by taking nude pictures of him.

She still hadn't decided on the best course when Monday dawned, the hour hands on her clock creeping slowly toward 6:00 p.m., when she'd have to be at After Hours to prepare the wet room.

TROY REHEARSED HIS SPEECH in the privacy of the Lotus on the way over. "Peggy, I realize that things look bad on the surface, but I never meant to lie to you. Yes, I made that first visit to the spa and even the second and third in order to find a way to break the lease, but I didn't plan on what happened between us. And later, I couldn't walk away from you...."

It was a start. He'd get her to see that he wasn't the jerk she thought he was. He'd make her understand. And then maybe she'd share this mud-bath thing with him. They'd get good and dirty together...yeah. Oh, yeah.

Really, when he thought about it, this plan of his was brilliant. And she'd started to soften, or she wouldn't have had him come in on a day when the spa was technically closed and nobody else would be there. She wanted a little privacy with him—that much was clear.

He pulled the Lotus into the parking lot and patted

her walnut steering wheel before he got out. Other ball players could keep their Lamborghini Diablos and their showy Porsches. He had a classy car.

Peggy's little blue Mini Cooper barely took up half a parking spot, and Troy reflected that it was the perfect car for her: compact and sporty with a sense of fun.

He knocked on the glass door of After Hours and she came out casually from the back, rolling up the sleeves of her white lab coat. Her hair was pulled back in a loose ponytail, and he was glad to see that it appeared Crisco free. Crazy woman. Adorable woman. His woman.

"Hi," she said as she unlocked the door. She was a little cool, but just the fact that she was speaking to him was a start in the right direction.

"Hi." He thought about kissing her, but it seemed like a bad idea. "Thanks for taking the appointment, especially on your day off."

She lifted an eyebrow. "It's not like you left me a lot of choice about seeing it through. Do you always threaten to sue women when they're already angry with you?"

Oh, boy. Perhaps a light approach was best? "Yes. I find that it mellows them, makes them more forgiving of jerks who've abused their trust."

She locked the door behind him. "Interesting."

"Peggy," he said. "In all seriousness, I was desperate to talk to you and you wouldn't let me near you. I didn't know what else to do."

"Troy Barrington, aka The Man, desperate?"

Groveling time. Women always wanted groveling. He wasn't particularly good at it, but for her he'd give it a whirl. "Yeah. Desperate. I've never met anyone like you before, and I don't want you to walk out of my life. Especially over a misunderstanding like this."

"Misunderstanding? Is that what you call the current situation?" Her tone was just short of scathing. She started walking toward the back of the spa, in the direction of the wet rooms. He followed.

"Peggy, what can I say besides I'm sorry?"

She reached the door of a wet room he hadn't seen before and opened it. Steam curled out: she obviously had already started the water and made her preparations.

Inside was a long, deep tub literally filled with a sloppy, liquid mud. The stuff looked disgusting. He viewed it dubiously, having second thoughts about any boinking in it. "I'm supposed to get *into* that?"

"Yes. It's a mineral-rich substance that's great in combination with steam for flushing toxins and impurities out of the skin. It will also relax your muscles. I'll set a timer for thirty minutes, and when you come out you can shower. Then I'll give you a twenty-minute massage. Okay?" Her voice was professional and detached.

"Any chance that you'll stay in here with me and we can talk?"

She looked at him wearily. "Troy, what is there to talk about? I have a long history of trust issues with men. You have lied to me since the day we met, and abused the trust that I stupidly placed in you. I hate liars and I hate feeling like a fool."

"I never lied to you. Omitting to tell you something

is not the same thing. And there were a number of times when I tried—"

"Get in the tub, Troy. I'm here out of professional obligation, and that's all."

"Please. I'm asking you to hear me out. Just give me five minutes."

She sighed. "Fine. I'll give you a couple of minutes to undress and then I'll be back."

He frowned at her. "It's not like you haven't seen everything there is to see."

She shrugged. "Leave your clothes in the locker room. They'll get damp from steam if they're in here."

He stripped off his shirt and unbuckled his pants on the way to the locker room door. He stepped out of them, dropped his drawers and kicked off his shoes. Troy left everything on a wooden bench and strolled back into the wet room. He looked down into the muck in the tub and wrinkled his nose.

"How do I know you haven't dropped a water moccasin or a piranha in there?" he asked Peggy.

She met his gaze levelly. "You don't."

He grinned. "That's my girl. Keep 'em guessing." He stuck a toe into the brown crap, and it actually felt silky and nice. He plunked his entire foot in, and when nothing bit it off, he stepped in all the way and sank down.

It was kind of like taking a bath in very rich hot chocolate, except the stuff smelled a little funky. Troy lay back in it and tried to relax.

"Is the temperature okay?" Peggy asked him. Her professional, polite tone was really starting to irk him.

"Yeah, it's fine." Then he added, "It would get hotter if you'd join me." He could rinse off this nasty stuff and they could get on with some good, clean fun....

Her expression told him that would happen when developers launched planned igloo communities in hell.

Hookay. "Look, regardless of my original nefarious intentions, I'm not going to break your lease here or try to boot you out of After Hours."

Her expression didn't change a bit.

"Doesn't that make you happy? Or at least bring us back to square one?"

Peggy exhaled audibly and gave him a derisive snort. "What, the emperor has granted clemency and now I'm supposed to kiss your ring?"

The only emperor he was familiar with was the one who'd worn no clothes. Which, he supposed, was apropos for the current situation, since he was butt naked, too. "Peggy, I've said I'm sorry. I've said I'm not breaking your lease. What else is there to say, except that I miss you?"

"I don't know what there is to say, except that everything between us is not okay. I am still mad and hurt and I still feel used. Those feelings are not going to disappear overnight. And I don't think I can ever trust you again." She got up. "Now, if you'll excuse me, I'm going to go get some clean towels." As she moved to the door, she inspected the waffle-weave robe that hung there. "This has a stain on it. I'll get another one of these, too." Then she dimmed the lights and disappeared.

Troy lay back in the hot slop and wondered how to

fix this. He refused to acknowledge defeat. He would find a way to make it up to her and make her happy.... The warm mud seeped into every crevice of his body, and he had to admit that it felt incredible. He laid his head back on the edge of the tub and nodded off.

When he awoke a few minutes later, the place was eerily quiet and his skin had pruned in the mud bath. "Peggy?" he called.

No answer.

"Peggy?" This time he yelled louder.

Silence.

Troy began to get a bad feeling. "Peggy!" he roared. Quickly he took stock of the room. Jars, bottles, CD player, CDs. No towels. She'd never returned with them as promised. No robe. Not even a box of tissues to dry off with.

Well, fine. He'd drain the slop in the tub, rinse off and find a towel in the locker room. Troy opened the drain and sat there while the mud gurgled down, leaving him brown, slimy and cold as well as naked. He turned the hot water tap on the tub, seeking relief.

Nothing happened.

He turned the cold water tap and got three small drips. The little redheaded witch had turned off the water main!

Troy stood and climbed out of the tub, eyeing the door to the locker rooms. She'd better not have... Dripping mud all over the tile floor, he sprang at the door handle and yanked hard.

It didn't budge. She'd locked his clothes in there!

His predicament began to hit home. Butt naked and

caked in mud, Troy let loose a stream of curses that would have made a sailor blush. He tore out of the wet room through the main door and looked around for something, anything, to cover himself. Didn't salons have those capes for customers to wear when they got their hair cut? He stalked around opening cabinets, but when he found the right one, labeled Smocks, the only thing it contained was a note in Peggy's handwriting. "Oops," was all it said.

"Witch!" he crumpled it up and threw it to the ground. She hadn't even left him a damned pillow. He was quite sure there was a pile of them sitting in a corner of the locker room, dead-bolted and secured. Even the phone was gone!

The only thing she'd left behind for him sat in the middle of the weird modern coffee table in the center of the reception area: his keys.

Troy looked outside at the cars whizzing by on the busy road, the people pulling into the parking lot to have dinner at Benito's. Peggy's car was noticeably absent. He looked at his own beautiful, freshly washed, waxed and detailed Lotus.

Then he looked down at his filthy, mud-encrusted, nude body.

He had two choices. He could stay here overnight, sleeping on the uncomfortable contemporary furniture and giving tomorrow's first employee an eyeful. Or he could grab a hair magazine to cover his privates and streak to his car.

Christ Almighty. He was going to open up a can of

whip ass on one little redhead when he caught up with her. And to think he'd actually come close to groveling!

He looked at the bizarre excuse for a couch that these people had. Serve them right if he slept on it and trashed it with the mud. But it was downright cold in here, and the thought of shivering in discomfort all night was not appealing. He figured he'd already gotten some measure of revenge, because Peggy was going to have a hell of a mess to clean up—his muddy footprints tracked all over the interior.

Troy grabbed his keys and a silly oversize hair magazine. Then, holding it in front of his crotch, he marched out the door. There was no turning back: the damn thing locked automatically behind him.

18

A FAMILY OF FOUR stared at him slack-jawed, the father rushing to cover up his little girl's eyes. A group of businessmen guffawed. The counter staff in the Arrowroot Café doubled over in mirth. Troy ignored them all, striding with purpose toward the Lotus.

He'd lovingly detailed her interior over the weekend and washed and waxed the exterior until she shone. He'd even conditioned the cream leather seats.

It just about killed him to sit on those seats in his filthy condition. He opened the door, hid his crotch behind it and placed the magazine strategically so that at least he wouldn't have a big muddy ass print on the driver's side. Bracing himself for the carnage, he slid inside and slapped his hands onto the wheel. He jammed the keys into the ignition, pushed in the clutch and started her up. Then he negotiated five of the ten minutes back to his house without incident.

He knew that he was in trouble the moment he saw the Miami-Dade squad car. He stared straight ahead, pretending utter nonchalance, as it pulled up next to him.

A black female police officer look a long, hard look

at him. She rolled down her window and leaned out, gesturing him to do the same. He complied, abject fear starting to beat a tattoo in his lower belly.

"Sir, are you all right?"

He gave her a wide, toothy grin. "Just fine, thank you, Officer."

"What is that all over you?"

Troy looked down. In the fading light of the sunset, the mud smeared on his chest looked rusty brown. "Oh, that. It's just, uh, mud. I slipped and fell on a…construction site." Please, God, let her swallow it and drive on.

She shot her partner a significant glance before turning back to him. "Sir, please pull over."

No! Dear God, please don't let this be happening. "I—uh, is there a problem, Officer?"

"Just a routine stop, sir. Now pull your vehicle over."

Troy weighed his options. If he gunned the Lotus, he had a small chance of outrunning them, even in the Miami traffic. But they'd still have his license plate number and would inevitably track him down.

If he pulled over and sprinted out of the car, they'd eventually catch him and then he could add charges of resisting arrest to a booking for public indecency. And when he was released? They could just add on a murder-one rap, because he was going to strangle Peggy Underwood with his bare hands.

Miserably, reluctantly, he pulled over.

The lady cop approached the driver's-side door and he instinctively put a hand over his privates.

"Hands on the wheel!" she roared.

Troy slapped his hand back over the polished walnut. *This is not happening…it's just not happening to me.*

Her footsteps came closer. Troy stared straight ahead, unable to even look at her.

"License and registration, please—oh, Lord have mercy! Where are your *clothes,* sir?" She spoke into her radio. "We've got us a streaker, here. Naked as the day he was born. Possibly covered in blood."

"It's not blood," Troy said. "I swear to you, it's mud! I fell on a construction site—" Too late, he realized that he shouldn't have lied. Now they definitely wouldn't believe the truth.

"License and registration, sir. *Now.*"

His wallet was in his pants. "I don't have any ID on me, ma'am. Somebody stole my clothes."

She put her hands on her hips and rolled her eyes. "Uh-huh. At the construction site, right?"

He swallowed.

"Where you were paradin' around in nothin' but a hard hat? Real nice, pervert. What's your name?"

"Barrington," he croaked. "Troy Barrington. Registration's in the glove box. Permission to open it?"

"Slowly. Keep your hands where I can see 'em."

"Ma'am, trust me, if I had a gun in there it'd be my own head I'd blow off." Troy reached over, opened the glove box and fished out his registration card. He handed it over. Had he been upset that nobody recognized him anymore? Now he thanked God and all His angels.

"But you don't have any photo ID on you."

"No, ma'am."

"What is your address?"

He told her. She wrote everything down. "Now step out of the car, please, sir."

Troy looked at the traffic backed up behind them, every driver looking bored and ready for entertainment. "Is that strictly necessary, Officer?"

"Step out of the car, sir! Don't make me ask you again." She cuffed his hands and ordered him into the back of the cruiser, where his bare butt immediately stuck to the warm vinyl seat.

The lady cop's partner took a long, disbelieving look at him. "Jesus Christ. Didn't you used to play strong safety for Jacksonville?"

Troy hunched his shoulders and kept his cuffed hands strategically placed. Had he really missed being recognized? Anonymity looked better and better.

The cop shook his head in disgust and spat out the window. He put the car into Drive and edged out into traffic. "Whose blood is that all over you?"

Troy gritted his teeth. "It's mud!"

God, he thought. *Just kill me now. Please. But do me a favor—take Peggy Underwood, too. You can drop her off with Satan at the portal to hell. They'll get along just great.*

PEGGY LAUGHED HERSELF sick on the way over to Marly's. She'd have one big mess to clean up early tomorrow morning, but it was so worth it.

She hoped Marly had ordered the deep-dish pizza and not the thin crust. It tasted so much better. She pulled up to her friend's condo complex and parked the

Mini, schlepping a bottle of red table wine with her as she made her way to the front doors. Marly's building, like almost every other one in Miami, was tall, vast and white. Some of the rooms overlooked the ocean and others overlooked a bunch of ugly warehouses.

Marly claimed she'd paid extra for the warehouse view, and draped the windows with sheer purple and scarlet curtains. This, combined with various exotic throws and cushions, made her living room look like a fantasy harem. Adding to the atmosphere were jeweled lanterns hanging from various architectural details. Marly placed tea lights in them and lit them whenever she was home.

Peggy thought it was quite the fire hazard, but refrained from comment.

She knocked on her friend's door, swinging the bottle of wine and feeling more cheerful than she had in days. Revenge had put her in a great mood.

Marly opened the door and yanked her inside. She looked flushed and excited. "Open the wine. I have something to celebrate."

"Me, too," said Peg. "But you first. What's your news?"

Marly produced a corkscrew and started the process of liberating their libations from the bottle. "I got a call from the governor's people today."

"Yeah? No kidding!"

"And I'm going to cut his hair tomorrow. At his hotel here in Miami. Can you believe that?"

"Good for you! And great for business." Peggy's smile faded as she thought about them having to move After

Hours. After her little stunt of today, it was a definite. She still didn't know how to tell Alejandro or Marly.

Impulse control, Peg. What happened to impulse control? Guess it went out the window along with the year of no men and the lentil salads.

Suddenly she was ashamed. It was one thing for her impulsive behavior to blow up in her own face. It was quite another for her lack of self-control to affect her friends' livelihoods. If she had just accepted Troy's apology…he'd said that he wouldn't break the lease. She wouldn't have had to date him. He wasn't *that* slimy.

"What's wrong?" Marly asked. "Why the long face?"

Peggy sighed. "I kind of did something today that I shouldn't have. Something that made me feel really good at first, but now makes me feel really bad."

She told Marly what had happened, glad that her friend's first impulse was to laugh. But then she looked devastated.

"We're going to have to move? What about all the remodeling, the huge loan, the fact that the clientele loves this location?"

"I know. God, I'm so sorry. I don't even know how to tell Alejandro."

"Can't we just get a retroactive permit for that tub or something?" Marly asked.

"Under normal circumstances we probably could. But these aren't normal. We're screwed." Peggy stared into her wineglass. "I guess it wasn't such a brilliant idea to offer me a partnership in After Hours. I've done more damage than good."

A couple of telling seconds went by before Marly jumped in with "Oh, that's not true."

Peggy met her eyes, her mouth twisting. "How am I going to tell Alejandro?"

The pizza arrived, rescuing Marly from having to answer. They ate it straight out of the box on the living-room floor, sitting cross-legged on big squishy pillows.

After a few minutes Marly put down her slice and wiped her fingers on a paper towel. "You can't tell Alejandro," she said. "He'll go into cardiac arrest. He's got his business school loans, the remodeling/build-out loan, the cash-flow issues and his executive MBA program on top of it all. His stress level is off the charts, and moving locations could damage us beyond repair—we'd have to close for six months just to get a new site ready.

"Peggy, you can't do this to him, you can't do this to yourself, and you can't do it to me. We have to figure out a way around this. Didn't you say that before your little stunt today, Troy was going to let us stay?"

The pizza now tasted like salty cardboard drenched in modeling glue. Peg nodded.

"Then you have to go find him and apologize. You have to make this right." Marly looked at her calmly.

Somehow Peggy managed to swallow. "You want me to tell him I'm sorry for getting even. After he's lied to me and used me and made a fool out of me."

"Do you see an alternative?" Marly's face still radiated beauty, despite her stern expression.

"No." Peggy's stomach roiled, and the wine she'd

poured down her throat now decided to try to make it back up, burning her esophagus.

"You know I love you, hon, but I don't see why Alejandro and I have to pay for your petty revenge."

"It wasn't petty!" Peggy jumped up and set down her glass on a side table.

"Okay, *petty* is the wrong word. *Infantile* is more apt." At Peggy's gasp, Marly got up, too, and took the pizza box into her kitchen. "The truth may hurt, but bankruptcy is going to hurt worse."

"I think I'll leave now." Peg headed for the door.

Marly came after her and caught her arm. "I know I'm being harsh right now, and I'm sorry for that. I hope this doesn't have to spoil either our friendship or our business relationship—but you have to make it right, okay?"

PEGGY DROVE BACK to After Hours with a mop, a bucket and a pair of bright yellow rubber gloves. She wanted to be furious with Marly, but when she looked at things from her partner's point of view, she couldn't blame her. Peggy herself would have said the same thing. Sometimes your friends had to tell you painful home truths.

Morose, she unlocked the door and relocked it after letting herself in. The place was an unholy mess: Troy had obviously looked everywhere for something to cover himself with before streaking to his car. She got to work with the mop, no longer finding the scenario funny.

Instead, what she'd done seemed small, mean and immature. Infantile, to use Marly's adjective. Still, a tiny part of her brain defended her actions. He'd been a total jerk to her and then compounded it by threatening to sue After Hours if she didn't agree to see him! He had *so* deserved her revenge.

But the other people in her life shouldn't have to pay for that revenge. *Impulse control, Peg. What the hell is wrong with you? Why couldn't you have thought it through? Realized the consequences of your actions?* She'd been utterly selfish.

If she were the only person affected by the issue, she wouldn't apologize to Troy Barrington if her life depended on it. But as she scrubbed mud off the floors of After Hours, cleaned the wet room and replaced all the things she'd locked away, she had to face facts.

And they added up to one thing: she needed to return his clothes and wallet to him and even kiss his feet, if necessary, so long as he agreed not to take out his anger on her friends.

Peggy folded Troy's clothes neatly, setting his watch and wallet on top of the pile. She took them out to the car with her, leaving the spa spotless. Nobody would be any the wiser in the morning.

The Mini's digital clock told her it was 9:30 p.m. She could drive to Barrington's house now, make the delivery and croak out her apology.

19

EVEN THE HOUSE looked mad at her. It squatted ominously at the end of Troy's cracked driveway, the windows seeming to squint at her, the door a tight frown.

Peggy gulped. She wondered if she should leave the Mini running in order to make a quick getaway, in case he came after her with murderous intentions.

She contemplated how she herself would feel toward someone who'd forced her to streak into a busy parking lot and drive home stark naked. Visions of steak knives, rat poison and vehicular homicide danced in her head. Perhaps this was not such a good idea…but she forced herself out of the car.

The front door opened before she'd taken two steps. Barrington stood there in a pair of faded Levi's, hands on his hips, his expression anything but welcoming.

"Crack a rib from laughing, did you?" he asked.

She caught her lower lip between her teeth. Then she just extended the pile of clothes.

"The least you can do is bring them all the way to the door. You were planning to dump them and run, weren't you?"

Her legs rooted to the ground, she shook her head. *Open mouth. Unstick tongue from roof of mouth. Form words. Push them out.* God, this was more hideous than she'd even imagined.

"S-s-sorry." She pushed the word out, but it was harder than forcing harmonious sound from a tuba.

Troy raised an eyebrow and eyed her with a considering, analytical expression. "No, you're not."

She furrowed her brow and glared at him. "Am, too." She pulled her feet from the imaginary quicksand sucking at them and made herself walk the remaining few steps. She extended the pile of clothes to him. "Here."

"Then I'm disappointed. Extremely so. The Peggy Underwood I used to know wouldn't have apologized if needles were being driven under her fingernails."

"Let me get this straight," she said slowly. "You're *disappointed* that I said I'm sorry."

"Yes. It ruins your entire revenge strategy."

"Look, Barrington," she said. "If it makes you feel any better, I'm not here on my own behalf. I'm here because my revenge screwed over my friends, my business partners."

"Ah. Now I understand. That's better. I begin to have some respect for you again."

Peggy's blood began to simmer. "Of course, I live for your respect."

He smiled. It wasn't a very nice smile. "Step carefully, Peggy-Sue."

She took a deep breath and counted to three. "Let me put it to you this way, Troy. Before I...pulled tonight's stunt, you indicated that you wouldn't break the lease and force us to move After Hours."

He nodded.

"I'm hoping that your decision hasn't changed. To be blunt, we have a huge loan that we took to pay for the build-out and remodeling of the spa. If we have to close for six months and reopen somewhere else, we'd lose all our business. We'd default on the loan. We'd all be financially ruined. I could handle that for myself, but I can't live with it happening to Alejandro and Marly, my partners. And there are staff and dependents involved, too."

"My heart bleeds," Troy said.

"Look, I can try to make this worth your while. I can pay you some extra money every month out of my salary. Just don't take out your anger on them."

"I'm not interested in your money."

This wasn't going well. But had she really expected it to? She had one last bargaining chip, but she didn't know how to even bring it up. She worked some saliva into her dry mouth. "Then what are you interested in, Troy?" She tried to inject her voice with a tinge of seduction.

A long, very long, pause ensued. She couldn't meet his eyes. When she finally did, his were hard and angry.

"Don't," he said. "Don't cheapen what we had." He dropped the pile of his belongings on the porch, took her by the shoulders and whirled her 180 degrees. Then he gave her a none-too-gentle shove. "Get out of here, Peggy. And don't come back."

TROY SLAMMED THE DOOR behind her, so hard that the walls of his hovel shook. He felt like destroying something. He was still furious with her over his very public humiliation and the fine he was going to have to pay on top of it all. Bad enough that people he didn't know had laughed at him, and that the police had, too. But Jerry had just about peed on himself when he'd come to get Troy out of jail. He hadn't chosen to share that part of his mortification with Miss Underhanded Underwood.

Troy was mad at her, mad at himself for making her mad at him and mad at Jerry for his mirth. In other words, he was a madman.

There was really nothing else in the kitchen for him to destroy. He prowled around the house, searching for something to take out his temper on. Screw anger management. Maybe he'd take a buzz saw to the old olive-green couch. Or burn the old geezer's plaid La-Z-Boy.

His eyes settled on the wall between the living room and dining room, a wall he planned to take out anyway. He'd half decided to liberate a sledgehammer from his toolbox in the garage when reason paid him a quick visit again. Best to find out if the wall was load bearing first. With a growl, he hunted down shorts, socks and some running shoes. Exercise was the only thing that would calm him down.

As he burned up the miles in the late-evening air, his aggression faded. He saw Peggy's face again as she'd stood before him, apologizing and resenting every second of it. A muscle had jumped in her jaw, her teeth were clenched and she'd elevated that little freckled nose of hers.

He grinned in spite of himself. That had cost her dearly. As a competitive spirit who enjoyed vengeance just as much as the next person, Troy knew it. But she'd come to grovel on behalf of the people she cared about, and that touched him.

He knew he was a big pushover, but he couldn't break the damn lease and kick them out. If that made him a bad businessman, so be it. As Peggy had stood there, attempting to hide her pugnacious attitude for her partners' sake, he'd fallen the rest of the way in love with her.

God *damn* it. Why he had to love a stubborn, freckled, bad-tempered little vixen he didn't know. One whom he should have shot on first sight. One who didn't want to be anyone's girlfriend and spent her days running her hands over other men.

Really, could he make a worse choice? He honestly didn't think so. The woman was so cynical she redefined the word, and she would undoubtedly drive him nuts and make his life a misery.

But she was also funny, sexy as hell and knew her football. She wasn't with him for the money or a borrowed identity. She challenged him at every step and she made love like there was no tomorrow.

Peggy Underwood was perfect for him. What other woman would have had the nerve to exact revenge on him the way she had? Troy started to laugh alone in the dark as he ran, aware that he was behaving even more like a madman. Well, tough. He was a madman in love.

PEGGY CLIMBED THE STAIRS to her apartment, so tired and depressed that she felt drunk. She gripped the iron railing set into the steps and used it to drag herself upward.

She unlocked the door, closed and relocked it behind her and slid down it into a heap on the floor. The silence shrieked at her, and the white walls gave her an instant headache. But Marly would probably never help her decorate now, since she'd let her down.

Peggy cringed as she pictured Alejandro's face when he heard the news. His dark eyebrows would draw together in a half incredulous, half furious squiggle; his eyes would snap with pure temper; his mouth would tighten in disappointment. He'd throw her out of the spa...but then what? Would he have to quit business school?

And Marly. In a flash of horror, she pictured her friend's beautiful tapestry pillows and candles inside a cardboard box by the side of the road. What would Marly do? She was a great hairdresser and could find another job in a heartbeat, but she'd lose her life savings.

Peggy started doing math in her head. If she sold her car, if she combined that money with what she had in savings and a 401(k) from when she'd worked for her brother, and if she borrowed a little from him, she could probably give Alejandro her part of the business loan. But it wouldn't make up for everything else: the lost income, the stress, the end of their friendship....

Peggy stared at the huge painted television on her wall, at the redheaded female kicker who'd just scored.

Her gaze was so intent on the ball that she'd lost focus on everything else around her.

The stadium crowd was a bunch of skillful blobs and dabs of color, details of a face here and there, courtesy of Marly's brush. The field—the ground that the kicker stood on—was a slash of green, hardly stable. And even the ball was beyond the figure's grasp, flying high through the air and through the goalposts to signify what? A point on a scoreboard? What exactly was the meaning of that?

It was fuzzy, not concrete, a fleeting blip on the radar screen of life. Worthless—similar to revenge.

Her eyes filled with tears. Troy had called innumerable times. He'd sent flowers. He'd brought chocolates. He'd tried reason and apology. What was it about her personality that made her so intractable, so tough to the point of stupidity?

He'd had to threaten to sue her just to get her to talk to him, and even then she hadn't listened. She'd just followed through with her idiotic plan of vengeance. She'd let her disappointment in her father and Eddie and her general cynicism twist her, somehow.

Was it possible that Troy had been telling the truth: that he'd had one goal when he first came into the salon, but had set it aside after meeting her?

Peg banged her hard head against the door. Well, she'd never know now, would she? She'd succeeded in ruining everything for everybody. She was a real winner, all right.

She didn't sleep more than two hours that night. She

lay there in the stark-white apartment bedroom, letting the sterility wash over her. She wished it would numb her thoughts, but instead the glaring white assumed the properties of noise and closed in on her, deafening and paralyzing.

When morning came she felt like a zombie, but her subconscious had sifted through all the possibilities of why she couldn't sleep. Yes, guilt and worry were part of the problem. But there was another looming issue, one that she wasn't sure she could grapple with right now.

She'd gone and fallen in love with Troy Barrington, the guy whose girlfriend she didn't want to be.

Peggy stumbled into the kitchen, made coffee and took a cup into the living room. Blearily she stared at Kicker Girl, the red hair streaming out from under the helmet she wore to protect her head. Stupid chick. Where was the helmet to protect her heart?

20

PEGGY STILL FELT like roadkill when she arrived around 8:00 a.m. at After Hours. It was her job to open this morning.

Her first client wouldn't show until eleven, so she unloaded some new supplies from their boxes and checked them in on the computer, doing her best to respond to Shirlie's chatter.

The receptionist had gone to a movie last night on a first date. "And then he spilled popcorn down my cleavage and tried to fish it out!"

"You're kidding," Peg murmured.

"No. I mean, how obvious can you get? I was like, 'Get out of my bra, thank you very much!'"

"So did he behave himself after that?"

Shirlie shook her head. "When he walked me to my door, he tried to vacuum my tongue out of my mouth. When's the last time a stranger tried to suck on your tongue?"

"Never, thank God." Peggy finished typing the last SKU number into the machine and hit Control and S to save the information.

"So gross. Then he tried to get into my apartment by claiming he had to use my bathroom. I told him it was broken and shut the door in his face." Shirlie brushed her hands together in a classic dusting-off gesture.

"Where did you meet this fabulous guy?"

"Over the avocados at the grocery store."

"Well," said Peggy. "Maybe you should try the fruit section next time. Peaches, maybe."

Shirl nodded. "You're telling me."

The door of the salon opened and in came Mel, their postman, with his cute little knobby knees hanging out of his regulation navy shorts. "Hello, my lovelies. Beautiful day, eh?"

"Hi, Mel. What's new?"

"Well, let's see. Newsflash! The sky is blue, the grass is green and my wife is shopping." He gave the same answer to the question every time they asked. "Now, what do I have here for you, my lovelies? Aha. This for Miss Underwood, looks terribly important and official." He handed an envelope to Peggy. "You'll have to sign for that, dearie, it's certified." He handed her a pen. "And a naughty lingerie catalogue for you, Miss Shirlie. Also some bills. The rest is for Tall, Dark and Handsome."

Peggy looked at the return address, which was a law firm's. Her heart dropped into her underwear. With a shaking hand, she signed for the letter and went into the kitchenette to open it privately.

Dear Ms. Underwood,

Pursuant to the matter of your business lease at 4915 Brickell Avenue, we ask that you appear at our offices at 11:00 a.m. on Thursday to discuss some issues regarding your tenancy at the property.

Please arrive at the following address promptly. We thank you in advance for your co-operation on this.

Very sincerely yours,

Jeremy Buckheimer,

Esquire

She ran over to the salon, where Marly was highlighting a customer's hair. The woman's head was piled with small squares of aluminum, and she was drinking a clear golden liquid from a coffee cup. Wine? At nine-thirty in the morning?

Peggy exchanged a glance with Marly, who just shrugged, as if to say that alcoholics had to have their hair done, too.

Peg waved the letter under Marly's nose. "Certified," she moaned. "Regarding you-know-what." Marly smiled angelically at the lady in her chair and set down her paintbrush and color bowl. "Will you excuse me for just a moment, Mrs. Dalton? I'll be right back."

She pulled Peggy to the other side of the salon. "You can't mention a word of this to Alejandro right now."

"But—"

"He's in the middle of exams! You can't."

Peggy took a deep breath. "Okay. But will you come with me? I have to go Thursday at eleven."

"I'm booked all day Thursday. Sorry, Peggo, but you're going to have to handle this alone. I thought you were going to apologize?"

"I did. It didn't do the slightest bit of good. I was even going to make an offer he couldn't refuse…but he did. He refused it before I could even get the words out! How unfair is that?"

Marly's large aqua eyes weren't devoid of sympathy, but they weren't forgiving, either. "You did make him streak to his car from the mud bath. I can't say I'd want to sleep with you, either, after that."

"Well, good. Because you're not my type."

"Go on Thursday and handle it like an—uh, like a pro. Apologize again if you have to. Just get us out of the soup."

Peggy had a strong suspicion that Marly had almost said, "Like an adult." Jeez, sometimes friends were tough. "Yeah. Out of the soup."

"Don't leave that letter lying around for Alejandro to find. I guarantee you he would freak and fail all his exams, and that's the last thing he needs."

"What would you like me to do with the letter, eat it?" Peggy stuffed it into her bra and walked away.

THURSDAY ARRIVED like a speeding bullet, even though Peggy would have preferred it to wait a month or two. She showered and then stood dripping in front of her closet, wondering how to dress appropriately for an eviction. Hair down or pulled up? Trousers or skirt? Scoop neck, V-neck or camisole under jacket?

She snorted at herself. Could anyone be more ridic-ulous? Finally she pulled a simple khaki skirt from its hanger and topped it with a white cotton blouse. She went for minimal makeup and close-toed chestnut sling backs. Pearls in her ears, a clip in her hair and a cinna-mon-mauve lip gloss completed the outfit.

She looked young, fresh and even a bit innocent. Weren't appearances deliciously deceiving?

Peggy pulled an ancient Vuitton signature bag from the back of her closet and dusted it off. Her father and stepmother had given it to her as a high school gradua-tion gift, along with the matching wallet. They couldn't have chosen anything less suited to her personality.

She tossed the matching wallet back into the closet and wrinkled her nose at the bag. But it was the only thing that came close to going with her shoes, and it seemed appropriately stuffy for a law firm. Besides, if you were going to be evicted, why not be tossed out with designer accessories?

Her stomach felt heavy and squeamish, as if it had big globs of mercury sliding back and forth inside. She popped some antacid pills and donned her most upscale Jackie O sunglasses. Then she walked toward the Mini and drove downtown to her doom.

Would she have to face Troy himself? Or just some faceless suit with a document? Probably the latter. Marly's words came back to her. "Handle it like a pro. Just get us out of the soup."

· Peggy had no idea how to handle this like a pro, other than bluffing her way through it. Maybe she should have consulted her own lawyer. But she decided to argue that they had indeed filed the permit for the mud bath plumbing. Obviously, it had just been misplaced.

She wondered wildly if she could bribe some city employee to "find" it. That always worked in the movies. The protagonist suavely slipped the guy an envelope and got his way. The audience forgave him his unethical behavior because they knew he was really a good guy.

I'm a good guy—er, good person. Why shouldn't I be able to pull this off? Peggy stopped for a light and fished her wallet out of the snooty Vuitton bag. A cursory review of its inner pocket revealed that she had nineteen dollars in ones. Not much of a bribe.

She dug into the Mini's console and discovered a pack of melted gum, three paper clips and some dusty change. She didn't have time to stop at a bank. So much for bribery. Though, come to think of it, the law firm would only be notifying her of the eviction today. Surely they had to give thirty to sixty days notice, and during that time she could produce the missing permit and fight back.

Peg parked in a vast garage that seemed to swallow her car the way a whale inhaled plankton. She hiked to the elevator and hit the button for the ground floor. Then she crossed the street to the office tower opposite the garage and took another elevator to the law firm's floor.

The mercury globs in her stomach slid back and

forth, her palms started sweating and she tamped down a rising hysteria. No! She was not going to lose it.

She pulled open one of a set of glass doors and introduced herself to a receptionist who looked like a runway model and had twice the attitude of one.

She was told to sit, like an obedient dog, until Mr. Buckheimer could see her. Fifteen minutes went by, during which Peggy figured she lost half her body's water content through her palms. At last a large, paunchy, jovial man came into the reception area.

"Miss Underwood! Pleasure to make your acquaintance. I'm Jerry Buckheimer. Hope you haven't been waiting long."

Peggy shook his big paw and wondered if he always looked so damn cheerful about evicting people. He radiated amusement, the sadist.

"Let me show you to the conference room, and then we can get started with the, uh, proceedings."

She ratcheted up her jaw, squared her shoulders and followed the man to a polished wooden door with glass panels to either side of it. The panels were hung with blinds, and these were drawn.

Buckheimer opened the door and ushered her in. A long cherry conference table greeted her, dotted with dozens of lit candles. A huge cut-crystal vase of irises sat in the center of it. And over the back of each chair around the table lay a pink numbered jersey. In each seat rested a pink football helmet and a pair of pink cleats.

Peggy stood there stupidly, taking it all in. Behind her

the door clicked shut and she turned to see Troy, hands in his pockets, leaning casually against it.

"Hi," he said.

She stared at him, her mouth working. "What are you doing here?"

"I was in the neighborhood," he said dryly.

"What, you came in for the kill?"

"Now, now."

She gestured toward the table, her expression a question. "Is there a kill? Or is this part of a sick joke?"

"I figured since you once thanked me for sending you flowers, that maybe I should give you some."

Peggy put a hand to her temple. "You, um, always give women flowers after they've played evil pranks on you?"

He nodded. "Yeah, especially when they get me arrested for indecent exposure."

Horrified, she clapped a hand over her mouth. "No... please tell me that didn't happen."

He nodded. "You couldn't have engineered it better, sweetheart. That mineral mud looks exactly like dried blood under a setting sun. Makes a driver *very* interesting to the cops."

He wasn't kidding. She tried to speak, but he cut her off. "I guess I now know exactly how you felt back in college, after the incident with those guys—the coach seeing you naked."

Her eyes flew to his and her mouth went dry. For a long moment she said nothing. Then she swallowed hard. "Troy, I am so sorry. What I did was beyond infantile, and I certainly didn't mean for—oh, God! No wonder you were so pissed when I showed up at your house."

"Let's just say that if this gets out, nobody's going to let me coach their little boys on a Pop Warner team."

She inhaled sharply; she hadn't thought of that. She looked at the floor while shame swallowed her. "And you're not strangling me *why?*"

"The thought did cross my mind once or twice," he admitted. "Okay, even three times. But I decided that was too easy."

"Too easy," she repeated. He was smiling at her. Why? And what was up with the flowers and the candles and the pink uniforms?

"Yeah. I want to torment you over a period of months, even years. Maybe decades, if you'll hang around that long and develop the right sadomasochistic tendencies."

She squinted at him. Was he saying what she thought he was saying?

"I can't strangle you," Troy explained, "because I fell for you the first night I saw you."

"You did?" Her insides started going gooey. Then she frowned. "That night in the parking lot? Wait a minute. You swore you weren't stalking me."

His mouth twisted and he caught his lip between his teeth. His eyes danced. "I wasn't stalking, exactly. But I *was* kind of spying. Playing Peeping Tom because I was convinced you guys at After Hours were giving more than massages in the back."

"*What?*"

"I was really disappointed when you weren't, since I could have broken the lease right away."

"You—you—"

"I thought you were real cute for a hooker." Troy grinned at her, dodging around the end of the table when she came at him, fist raised. "I wondered what you looked like under that lab coat."

She dropped the Vuitton bag on the floor, snarled and leaped over it. Then she tackled him.

Unfortunately, as he'd argued during their discussion about coed football, her 120-pound body was no match for his 230-pound one. He laughed as she head-butted him and tried to knock him off balance. Then he picked her up and held her at arm's length while she flailed her hands and feet. *"Hooker?"* she panted.

"What was I supposed to think, when After Hours was open until midnight and you were serving alcohol? I found it highly suspicious."

"You are *unbelievable!*"

"If it's any consolation, you forced me to consider paid sex for the first time in my life."

"Oh!" She tried to head-butt him again. "Put me down, you bastard, so I can kill you."

He shook his head. "So, you see, I deserved your revenge the other night more than you knew."

She hissed at him.

"I thought that might make you feel better."

"Oh, trust me. It does."

"Okay. Is it safe to put you down now? You really shouldn't try to harm the guy who's bought your entire powder-puff team pink athletic gear. Expensive gear, I might add."

She turned her head to look at it.

"Doesn't that count for something?"

Grudgingly, she nodded.

"Okay." He set her on her feet.

"Why did you do that? Get the gear?"

"Well, it's along the same lines of why I can't strangle you. I'm awfully afraid that I've developed feelings for you."

"You have?"

"Uh-huh."

"What kind of feelings?" she asked cautiously.

"Mushy ones. The kind that warp my normally clear logic and bring me to strange conclusions. Like being charmed when a woman puts Crisco in her hair and sprays her T-shirt with Raid in the hopes of not being my girlfriend."

"Really? You thought that was charming?"

"No. I said I was charmed by it. The behavior itself borders on psychotic, but let's not discuss that right now, okay?"

She took a step closer and peered up at him. "What would you rather discuss?"

He cocked his head and smiled down at her, touching her hair. "Breaking and entering."

Now she was really confused. "That's illegal."

"Not in this case," he said, cupping her chin. "You promise not to break my heart, and I promise not to break your lease. We enter into an agreement."

She smiled, but he stole it with his lips. They were warm and insistent, parting hers and taking possession of her mouth. He kissed her for long moments before finally lifting his head. "So what do you say?"

"I say we have a deal—on two conditions."

"What's that?" He nuzzled her neck.

"First of all, you can't break *my* heart, either. Second, you agree to a match between my powder-puff team and your boys. We're gonna whip your butts, pink helmets and all!"

"Done," he said promptly. "Name the time and place. We'll wipe the field with you. Now, are you my girlfriend again?"

She chewed a fingernail and thought about it. "Do we have to use that word?"

"Well, you got all upset when I offered alternatives," Troy said, throwing up his hands. "There's no pleasing you."

"Okay, okay." Peggy took a deep breath. "I think I'm in love with you. So it sucks…but I am your girlfriend."

Epilogue

TROY SWELLED with satisfaction, opening and closing his fists inside his light-blue windbreaker. Blue for boys. As opposed to all those pink jerseys running around out there on the playing field over pink cleats.

Thank God his team wasn't getting humiliated by Peggy's girls: it was the one thing he couldn't handle. She stood on the sidelines opposite him, her little freckled face grim with determination. The score was twenty to fifteen, in the boys' favor. With difficulty, Troy refrained from inserting his thumbs into his ears and waggling his fingers at her, humming, "Nah, nah-nah-nah nah!" He strove for maturity; he was superior simply by being male and didn't need to rub it in.

Twenty-three seconds left on the clock, and his boys had the ball on their own seventeen-yard line. He told Derek to deliver the message when they huddled: "It's the second down, kids. The other team has no time-outs left, remember? So all you have to do is snap the ball and take a knee. Go get 'em!" He fairly danced in anticipation, grinning like a monkey. Peggy would never live this down, after all her taunts about the girls wiping the field with them. Nah, nah-nah-nah nah! His girl-friend owed him dinner and a bl—

"No!" he yelled in disbelief. The little peckerheads had muffed the snap! There was a bad exchange between the center and the quarterback; the quarterback fumbled the ball and it *hit the ground, with one of the pink jerseys diving on top of it.* No! Damn it, that was a turnover.

Peggy took a turn grinning like a monkey, now. She jumped up and down and screamed, her red ponytail flying through the air. *"Yes!* Girl Power!"

Girl Power, my hairy ass. But the damn pinkos had the ball on the fifteen-yard line now. *Keep it away from Danni,* Troy prayed. *She's the menace.* "Defense!" he roared.

His boys did the best they could; he had to give them that. But the prissy little pink jerseys got the ball to his niece and blocked Derek when he tried to mow his sister down. Danni sneered at him as she threw a perfect twenty-yard spiral right into the end zone. The touchdown was complete, bringing the score to 21-20, girls' favor.

Laura added insult to injury when she kicked the final point after touchdown, upping the pink score to twenty-two.

Peggy ran onto the field, still screaming in excitement, and hugged every single little girl out there as Troy tried to restrain a deep, moody growl. Girls didn't beat boys. They just didn't. Not at football. Not when even their flippin' little toenails were painted pink. Couldn't they be burly and have budding beards, so he could comfort himself by speculating that they'd had a sex change? But they were just as feminine and cute as they could be.

He walked out on the field, too, to comfort his kiddos. "We'll get them next time, but good," he promised.

"Yeah, get us burgers, maybe!" Peggy gloated.

"Coach Underwood," he warned, "am I going to have to teach you a lesson on good sportsmanship when we get home?"

"I don't know, Coach Barrington. Does it still involve—" she leaned forward to whisper in his ear "—handcuffs and hot baby oil?"

"As I recall, it does indeed."

She flashed him a wide, naughty grin and said her next words at full volume. "Well, then, boys, I think you'll be needing to fetch us some sodas with those burgers—and wash our dirty uniforms, too!"

* * * * *

Look for the continuation of the
AFTER HOURS *miniseries!*
Karen Kendall delivers Marly's story in
MIDNIGHT MADNESS,
coming May 2006 from Harlequin Blaze.

What are *your* forbidden fantasies?

Samantha Sawyer is a photographer who's
dying to live out her sexual fantasies....
The tricky part is her new assistant
has morphed into her dream man.
And once he's tempted,
there's no going back....

DON'T TEMPT ME
by *Dawn Atkins*
On sale May 2006

UNCUT

Even more passion for your reading pleasure!

You'll find the drama, the emotion, the international settings and the happy endings that you love in Harlequin Presents. But we've turned up the thermostat a little, so that the relationships really sizzle.... Careful, they're almost too hot to handle!

Are you ready?

"Captive in His Bed weaves together romance, passion, action adventure and espionage into one thrilling story that will keep you turning the pages...Sandra Marton does not disappoint."
—Shannon Short, *Romantic Times BOOKclub*

CAPTIVE IN HIS BED
by Sandra Marton

on sale May 2006

*Look out for the next thrilling
Knight brothers story, coming in July!*

If you enjoyed what you just read,
then we've got an offer you can't resist!

Take 2 bestselling love stories FREE!
Plus get a FREE surprise gift!

With these women, being single never means being alone

Lauren, a divorced empty nester, has tricked her editor into thinking she is a twentysomething girl living the single life. As research for her successful column, she hits the bars, bistros, concerts and lingerie shops with her close friends. When her job requires her to make a live television appearance, can she keep her true identity a secret?

The Single Life
by Liz Wood